# Charmed in
# CHESHIRE BAY

USA TODAY BESTSELLING AUTHOR
## H.M. SHANDER

# Table of Contents

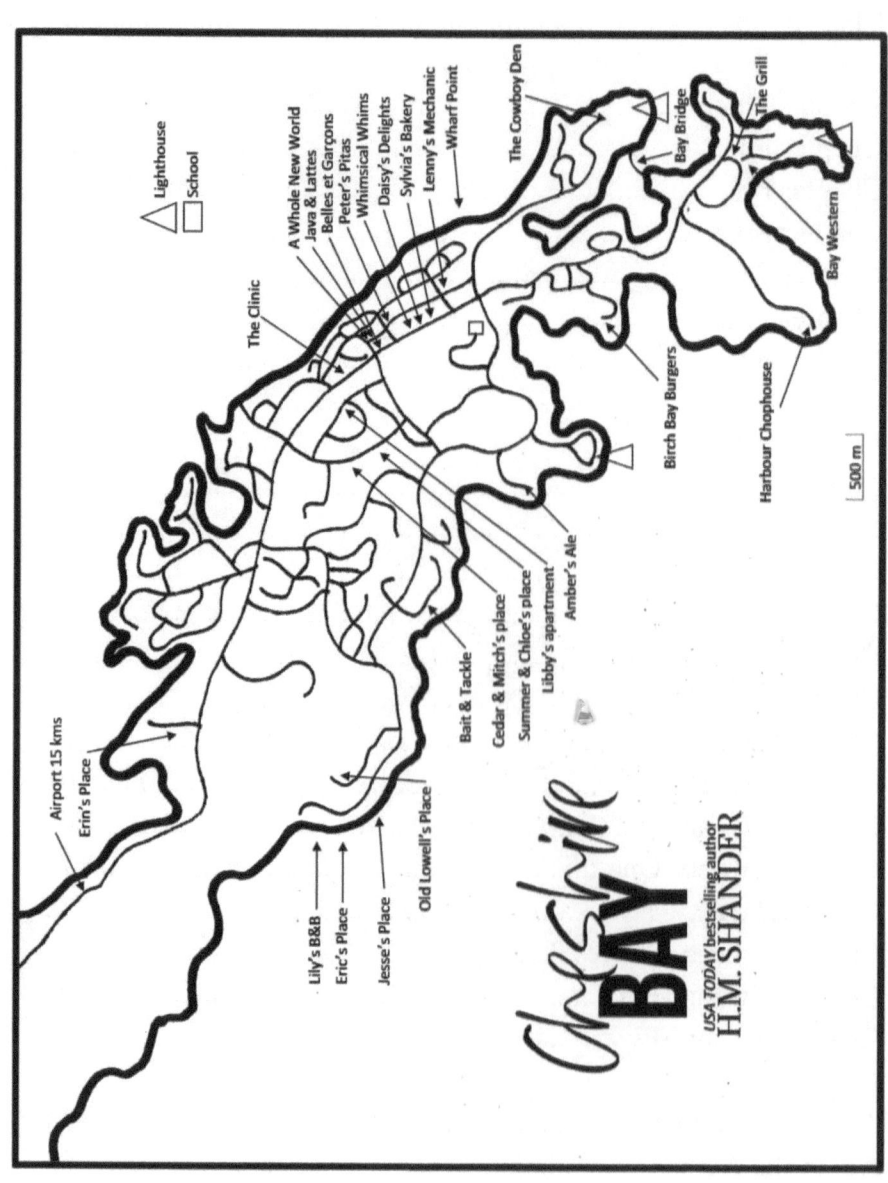

Cheshire
BAY
USA TODAY bestselling author
H.M. SHANDER

Lighthouse
School

A Whole New World
Java & Lattes
Belles et Garçons
Peter's Pitas
Whimsical Whims
Daisy's Delights
Sylvia's Bakery
Lenny's Mechanic
Wharf Point

The Clinic

The Cowboy Den
Bay Bridge
The Grill
Bay Western

Birch Bay Burgers
Harbour Chophouse

500 m

Airport 15 kms
Erin's Place

Lilly's B&B
Eric's Place
Jesse's Place
Old Lowell's Place

Bait & Tackle
Cedar & Mitch's place
Summer & Chloe's place
Libby's apartment
Amber's Ale

# Chapter One

I rolled over and smacked into the hard *naked* and deeply muscled back, startling myself into sobriety as I came to in a flash.

Shit! What had I done?

A groan filled the space for a heartbeat, only to be replaced by the deep, placating sound of a soft snore.

Blinking faster than my heart pounded, I slowly inched out from under the thin sheet providing the only cover and patted the darkened edge of the bed for my clothes.

What had I worn again?

Oh right, a cashmere sweater and skinny jeans; two things that shouldn't be hard to feel for. Pushing my ratty hair into a makeshift bun, I slithered off the bed and onto the cool of the hardwood floors, crawling like a baby with my naked ass high in the air. My fingertips grazed the soft feel of cashmere as a grunt came from the sleeping stranger. Instinctively, I froze as my heart stopped dead. When the snoring resumed, I quietly pulled the high-end sweater over my bare chest and carried on with my gentle floor tapping, hoping some sort of magic would assist in locating my jeans. Was pretty sure my panties and bra were never going to be found. Not like this. Not without a light of some sort. And a clearer head.

Holy shit, how much had I had to drink?

Almost resigned to wearing the sweater as a barely-there minidress, lady luck entered the blackened room and pushed the jeans into my path. Holding my breath so ripe I winced, I slipped into the legs, leaving them unzipped. I could finish that outside. At least I was covered.

Tiptoeing like my life depended on it, I exited the bedroom in five long strides, and found the door and my Coach knockoff, but only when I kicked it into the wall. Yanking it off the floor and holding it close to my chest, I listened to ensure I was alone and that the guy was still snoring.

Success.

Inhaling slowly and rhythmically in a dire attempt to control the rush of adrenaline and the stench of sexy body sweat, I twisted the knob and opened the door just enough to slip through into the cool midnight air.

Closing it tight behind me, I sighed and covered my eyes in my brightly lit surroundings, giving myself a breath or two to get used to the total one-eighty in light. As I blinked in the glow of the streetlights, the area was as unfamiliar to me as the darkened room I'd just exited. Far off in the distance, a horn sounded, like the kind from a cruise ship, long and deep. Right. I was somewhere in

Cheshire Bay. A town I'd only moved into yesterday.

What a welcome. My roommate and best friend, Chloe, helped me party way too hard at some hillbilly hangout. I vaguely remember the dashing cowboy who I'd drunkenly attached myself to and swore I'd dance with until they kicked us out. Guess the dance party continued at his place.

Drunk me was always at a loss of sanity. I'd likely give away the security code to my former office building if I could remember it since irrationality consumed me harder than the liquor. At least I didn't turn violent with my inebriation. Rather, I turned into a version of a horny teenager, ready to bed anyone, evident by the sleeping stranger on the other side of the wall.

The ocean breeze blew my once wispy waves into my face, blinding me temporarily. As I cleared my vision, I spied a set of metal stairs and raced down them as lightly as I could. My quads and knees were going to kill me from the painstaking movements of not daring to make any indication of descent.

My bare feet hit the cool of the asphalt, as in my immediate haste I'd never even bothered searching for my footwear, and I moved along the sidewalk like a tramp. In my condition, it wasn't far off; barefooted, no jacket, with hair askew and my mascara making clumpy specks in my vision. Wandering aimlessly, I finally found a street name that sounded familiar. Main Street.

My apartment wasn't too far away. Chloe and I had just moved into the U-plex in the middle of town – a "U" shaped building with a riveting sight of the other side of the wraparound complex.

Room with a view was our only motto when we travelled.

Chloe had mentioned it would only take me a day to memorize the town of 2500, and two days to remember all the residents. I truly hoped not. No one needed to remember this. Or me.

Shivering, I managed to walk along the grassy sections until I spotted our walk-up. Relief washed over me, and I made my way inside, only to crash on top of my still unmade bed after praying no one would remember me. This wasn't the way I needed to be thought of.

After a solid death-consumed-me type of sleep, I showered and turned myself into Miss Professional. Today, I was going out to make short work of memorizing the town and checking out which stores I could potentially ask to join the Bayside Market as a vendor – my newest endeavour. In my research, I discovered the area did not have a farmer's market type of event, odd given the location and demographics, and yet with all the small-town charm and homemade goodies, a market could have a plethora of unique offerings for the upcoming tourist season. I'd already created the website, drawn up contracts, and secured a location for the weekly event, all before having moved into Cheshire Bay. All I needed were vendors. Many of them.

Cheshire Bay sure looked different in the warm glow of a beautiful spring morning. The main drag was teaming with life, and the townsfolk mingled outside the storefronts, smiles painted on their faces, as they slid open grated doors and set items outside their windows. The air was crisp with the scent of fresh flowers, and as I meandered through the town, it was hard to not pick up on the infectious feeling of joy. The main street was picturesque, like a real-life Hallmark movie, and stores with the most fun names dotted the view. Names like *Daisy's Delights, Sylvia's Bakery,* and *Whimsical Whims* were the first places I'd stopped at this morning, easily adding them to the list of booked vendors. Everyone was so warm and welcoming. I'd only been in town for twenty-four hours and already it felt like home.

One of my final stops of the day was the local bookstore - *A Whole New World* – a brick building tucked on the road behind Main Street. Bells chimed overhead as I pushed open the heavy door, and instantly a sweet aroma like vanilla or buttercream filled my senses. The scent put me at ease, probably part of the owner's plan, something about the power of gentle smell tickling the positive memories tucked into the back of the mind. Who doesn't love a cozy little bookstore?

"Welcome," a male voice called out, although I saw no one. "Help yourself, and if you need anything, just holler."

"Okay," I said into the air, still unsure of where the voice had come from.

My first plan of action was to survey the goods, and see if there was something that would appeal to tourists.

I glanced around the brightly lit interior, filled with shelves of books and artfully decorated signs. Bestsellers were perched in the storefront window display, books by renowned authors like James Patterson, BJ Sutcliff, and Emma Tharp.

The deeper I ambled through, the more I started looking at the titles of the books. The bindings had changed, from bright and colourful with fun fonts, to dark and monotone, typically with gold lettering. Clearly, I had stepped into the ancient book section. And where tourists were concerned, they probably wanted something more local, or a good page-turning beach read. The ancient tomes weren't quite what I had in mind.

A voice sprang up behind me. "Looking for anything in particular?"

My hand flew to my chest as my heart skipped a beat since I hadn't even heard him approach. The voice belonged to a handsome young guy, someone who couldn't have five years on me. But it wasn't his youthfulness that caused the breath to escape my body and my heart to stop beating.

"It's you." His dark blue eyes narrowed slightly and darkened. "The escape artist."

# Chapter Two

y sexy cowboy looked completely different in the glow of the midday morning, and it wasn't just because he was devoid of his cowboy hat and giant belt buckle. He was tall, gorgeous with dark blue eyes, and a hint of stubble on his chin. Seeing him in a fresh light changed nothing, my body remembered and responded in kind.

Avoiding the giant elephant in the room, I inhaled, and jump-started my heart with a hearty cough. "I'm here to pick up a friend's book. She had it on order or something?"

He gave me a small nod and walked behind the counter. A long finger tapped on the computer. "Name?"

"Summer Bates." It was a force of habit and my own name fell out so easily. Too easy most of the time. Heat seared my cheeks like flames on a log. "Oh, you mean my friend?"

At least it earned me a sly smile, the kind that crinkled the edges of his deep blue eyes. "Yes, please."

"She's Chloe Tarkin."

"Ah, yes, the new doctor in town."

"That's her."

Chloe had mentioned how small some towns were. Point in case.

"That makes you her best friend?"

I pulled my shoulders back and shook the bangs out of my face. "Yes, it does."

The smile deepened, and with it, my heartbeat raced to epic levels. He cleared his throat. "I guess we never got formally introduced last night."

The metaphorical elephant stomped around the bookstore.

With a quick nod, he grabbed a nearby coil-bound book. "Pleased to meet you, Summer. I'm Adam, and when Chloe told me to expect you today or tomorrow, I had no idea we would've already met."

Had Chloe known last night who the cowboy was? Surely, she must've. She'd been in town two weeks previous.

My mouth went dry as cotton. "Yeah, about that?"

"It's all good."

"It is?" Why didn't I believe that?

"Sure. We had a good time last night, a real good time, and you ghosted me. It's pretty clear to me."

Now I was confused, but I glanced quickly around the space to ensure we were alone. "What exactly is *pretty clear*?"

"Look, I'm not stupid, okay? You got what you wanted, and

you left." A soft snort blew out of him, and he angled himself away from me.

Ohmygod, was he playing the victim? Was he devastated I didn't stick around for breakfast or something? Holy smokes. What kind of town was this?

I blinked rapidly and took a solid look at the guy, easily putting his looks at a nine, although his clipped tone was lowering it a notch.

"Last night was not me, not the real me. You saw the party part I haven't been able to ditch since high school, although she doesn't make an appearance all too often." Unless copious amounts of cheap, hard liquor were involved. One-dollar shooters were obviously part of my undoing.

"You talk about her like she's someone else. Another personality."

My eyes widened with surprise and a wild sense of relief. "Yes, exactly like that. Normally, this is me. Prim and professional."

I waved my hands over my put-together self. Clean skinny jeans, a gorgeous sweater that cost far too much normally but was just the right price when it went to the sale rack, boots in a nice tan colour that paired nicely, and hair and makeup done like I was out for business, and not for a night on the town. I even spun around for good measure and tossed my hands out to the side.

A good-natured laugh filled the space, but his cheeks tinted a faint blush colour. "Nice." He leaned on the countertop and gave me a head-tilting stare. "Speaking of professional, Chloe mentioned her best friend was going to drop by to pick up her book, and because you were on the prowl for business, you'd likely want to talk to me about my business. However," he rose and rubbed his chin, "she never said what it is you do."

I composed myself and pulled confidence and information from the rational part of my brain still somehow firing on all cylinders. "I'm an event coordinator, and I'm in the process of setting up Bayside Market, a weekly farmer's market type of event."

"Oh, well, that's great. Not sure how that would involve me." His tone dropped, and without much interest, he turned away, grabbing a book off the back counter with a bright yellow sticky on it, and pushed it toward me. "Here's her book."

Having known Chloe for years, the title seemed completely out of character for her. "This is the correct book?"

He typed on the computer and gave it a quick read. "Yep, sure is."

"And it's paid for?"

"In full." He removed the sticky note and crumbled it.

I took Chloe's book and quickly tossed it into my bag, a little perplexed at why she'd order one on Kama Sutra; she didn't even have a boyfriend. "Anyway, back to the Bayside Market idea, are you the owner?"

"Owner, employee, and caretaker." He nodded with a wink and a grin that pushed up on the left side of his handsome face. Surprisingly, it had the power to weaken my knees a tad.

"Must be a helluva Christmas party."

With that, he tossed his head back as he laughed. "That's one I've never heard before." He reached out his hand, which I shook in return. "Chloe speaks highly of you and said how funny you are. It's nice to be formally acquainted."

"A frequent visitor, is she?"

"She is. So, tell me, Summer – great name by the way – what do you have in mind for the Bayside Market, and how does it involve me?"

I produced a folder I'd spent way too much on and set it between us. It had my newly developed logo, and I was quite pleased with how it looked; it gave a professional edge to a fresh, unestablished business.

"Inside contains all the information, with a link to the website where you can fill out your contract and submit your first two vendor rental payments."

Adam opened the folder and pulled out the thick packet, causally flipping through the many pages, his long fingers holding it firmly and yet, cautiously, like it was a rare, antique book. "It's very detailed."

"Thank you." I'd put a lot of time and effort into creating it, pulling from information packages I used to hand out in my former business.

"What would you like of me though? How would this market benefit my business?" He leaned on the counter to level himself with me and made hard eye contact.

"Well…" Since this stop had been an unplanned business

trip, I hadn't taken the time to mentally prepare for an interview of sorts. Now I was going to have to wing it. The area was ripe with devastating possibilities. "For instance, you could bring a selection of books and bookmarks. We're going to be set up in the parking lot alongside Hardy Beach, near the airport."

"So, you're saying I'll likely need more beach reads." His fingers skimmed his jawline, giving his slightly stubble-covered chin a rub.

"Whatever you think the beachgoers and tourists would like. I'm providing the location, it's up to you to decide what to bring."

"Commitment time?"

"I know it would be hard to commit to all twenty-two weeks of the market, but if you can commit to half, that would be great. Customers love the consistency of knowing their regular vendors will be on site."

"Locals don't visit Hardy Beach, but yes, the tourists flock there in droves. It's a great location for a market. Well done."

My eyes widened at his statement. It was only the best beach on this section of the big island. All the tour guides rated it #1 and that's why I forked out a huge loan to rent space weekly there until mid-October.

"Hardy Beach is too crowded for us locals. However, if you're interested, being how you're new in town, I can give you a tour and show off where the best-hidden gems are." He ran a fingertip along the creased edge of the folder, but it was his smoldering gaze drawing my attention. "They're not places you'll find in Frommer's or Fodor's or even the Lonely Planet Guide."

Despite my racing heart, I broke the connection and stared at my market packet, my voice cracking as I spoke. "Sure, I'd like that."

That sweet grin settled back on his face. "Perfect. It's a date. Does tomorrow work?"

I stumbled over my words, and grimaced, taking a step backwards. "As long as we don't actually classify it as a date."

"Okay?" His voice pitched, and he tipped his head to the side. "You have a different word?"

"Meeting? Tour? Get together?"

He slowly nodded and gave me the once over as if he just realised I was slightly unbalanced and the best way to move forward was cautiously. "Fine, I'll rephrase. Would you be interested in a tour of the local hidden gems?"

Saying no wasn't really in my best interest, since as a business deal, I worried turning down his offer would negatively affect his signing an eleven-week contract. I could really use the money and needed all the contracted vendors I could book. I hadn't even started it yet and was already deeply in the red.

"No strings attached?" A bad habit from my previous line of work. It was a lot of *scratch my back, I'll scratch yours* kind of business. And I hated it.

"No." He tipped his head to the side, his words coming out nice and slow. "No strings attached."

"Perfect." I nearly curtsied in gratitude and breathed out a shallow exhale. "How about Monday? Would that work?"

"I close at four, and it's dark by 7:30, but sure, that'll give us a few hours to see some of the sights."

"I thought Cheshire Bay was small?"

"It is, but the bay area itself is quite expanse. There are some real beauties around these parts."

Based on the way he gazed into my eyes, I could've sworn he was talking about me. Then, rationally, I returned to thinking like a normal person and figured he was just in love with this village. Either that, or he was desperately lonely, which was impossible since he was stunning and charming. Yep, had to be his deep love of the area.

"Meet you here for four?"

He nodded and pulled himself up to his full height. "That's fair."

I patted my bag. "Thanks for the book. Give the package a read over and we can discuss any questions on Monday."

"Looking forward to it. Have a good day, Summer."

"You as well, Adam."

At least I had made my policy on my self-imposed no-dating rule clear. Yep, I stumbled around and got defensive, but it was all for the best. I wasn't in Cheshire Bay to date or fall in love with a devilishly handsome cowboy. I was here to make a name for myself, on my own merits with nothing shady in the background, and to show the world how I didn't need to depend on anyone because no matter what they said, they were willing to dump on you and let you down.

# Chapter Three

hloe's hand shot up and waved me over, so I walked with undivided purpose to the booth she was sitting in. I'd half expected a fast-food place, but Birch Bay Burgers was a giant step up from that with its light interior, plethora of greenery, and deep comfy seats - no hard plastic chairs here. It was equivalent to some higher end places my former company would take clients.

Before I sat, I retrieved the book she'd asked me to pick up and set it on the edge of the table, waiting for her to snatch it up quickly and hide it away. Instead, she left it there for any and all to see.

"Thanks for getting this."

"Yeah, you're welcome." I scooted into my seat and opened the menu. Yep, definitely higher end; this was no fast-food chain. Mind you, I hadn't noticed any national chains of any kind, which was nice, part of that small-town charm and appeal. "Oh, by the way, I met the bookstore owner."

Even though I hadn't lifted my gaze from the words on the menu, it wasn't hard to miss her smile. Infectious, it had the ability to light up a room and just seeing it, had a pleasant effect.

"And?" She closed her menu and leaned closer.

"And what?"

Our server appeared, interrupting our conversation.

Once he was out of earshot with our drink order, she spoke. "He's nice, isn't he, the bookshop guy?" Chloe leaned against the back of the booth. "Kind of dreamy."

I gave her a hard stare, daring the giggle of knowing the truth to burst out of her. Nothing happened. "You recognized him, right?"

"Of course, he lives here. He runs the bookstore." Her head tipped. Clearly, she had no idea.

"Last night? He was the cowboy."

"That was him? Get out." Her doe-eyed browns got smaller as the size of her whites grew. "He looks so different. Wow. Adam doesn't seem the cowboy type. He's more…"

"Laid back?" The calm guy in the bookstore was a far cry from the boisterous cowboy boot-scooting around the bar.

"I was going to say boring, but, meh, laid back works too."

"He's very friendly." No doubt, it was part of the job to a small degree, although some are born with charisma, and some are not. Adam was clearly in the first category, as his grin had the ability to make my heart race just a touch faster than should be respectable.

"Okay. If you say so."

I gave a hard look to my best friend and closed my menu.

Everything looked good, so I'd take whatever our server suggested. "What precisely are you getting at?"

"He's mid-thirties, single. Recently divorced. He's been running the bookstore for a while and has lived here all his life."

"Someone's done her homework." She probably figured out where he lived too, although as I thought about it, *I* wasn't even sure where he lived. But it was close to the bookstore and Main Street, that much I remembered.

"Maybe he's looking for a little big-city girl action."

I laughed. "Me?"

"Absolutely. You're a stranger who just happens to be alluring to boot. Who knows what could happen? Do you think you'll be a frequent visitor to the store?" She wiggled her eyebrows as she waited for the answer I'd need to choose my words carefully for.

If I said the wrong thing, she would use it against me. Lovingly, of course. Thank God she wasn't aware of last night's indiscretions, since I'd snuck in before she woke up.

"He does have the package I give my vendors, so perhaps." Although I wouldn't complain about gazing into those dark blues of his again. But just look, no more touching. That was off the table.

"So, you'll be seeing him soon?"

I shrugged, and debated not saying anything further, but then, this was my best friend – I'd never kept much from her before. "We're going to meet on Monday."

"I knew it." Chloe smacked the menu with enthusiasm.

I crossed my legs. "It's all business, so take it down a notch.

We're going to discuss the market, and he's going to show me some local treasures – as my tour guide."

"Look at you, you've been here less than twenty-six hours," she checked her watch for good measure, "and you already have a date. I've been here for two weeks and haven't had much in the way of stimulating male interaction." She pouted, her plump lip rolling out.

Rather than focus on the word *date,* I eyed the book flashing like a bright neon on the table's edge. "Is that a subtle hint to any passersby?"

"It's an invitation, and I wouldn't turn down a little fun. A girl's gotta live, right?"

No sooner had she spoken when our server stopped by with our drinks. He paused a little too long to be just a friendly staff member, and he gave a wink to Chloe. After she bobbed her straw in her diet coke and eyed him seductively, he took off.

I cleared my throat. "Isn't he a little young?"

"He's clearly of legal age since he served a table over there a round of beers."

"Yeah, *just* legal. He's like ten years younger than you."

"Still… imagine the stamina." She turned and searched him out. "Ah, but you're right. Probably lives at home with his mommy."

"And maybe finishing up high school." Figured I throw in a dig where I could. "Why don't you go out with Mr. Bookworm?"

"Who says I haven't tried?"

"What?" I nearly choked on my drink.

"Well, he wasn't taking what I offered, and I wasn't being too subtle either."

"So naturally you figured he was my type."

She shrugged, tossing a shoulder into the air. "Maybe. Or he'll help you over…"

A long painful pause hung in the air. Because Chloe didn't know the complete truth about why I'd packed everything up and followed her, she could be assuming I needed help in getting over Declan. Which was true, but not in the way she thought. I needed therapy, a lawyer, and more to get over him, nothing a guy like Adam could help with.

Then there was Andre, my fiancé from a few years back who fought cancer and lost. He'd been my only love, despite the world thinking Declan had stepped up to replace Andre, but if they only knew the truth. I vowed I'd never have another relationship again. Too many issues. Way too much heartache and knocks to the mental health.

"Anyway," Chloe lifted her glass and held it near mine. "To new beginnings."

I clanked my drink against hers, ready to fully embrace a fresh start. "To new beginnings."

That's what the move to Cheshire Bay was all about.

Starting fresh. Making a name of my own. On my own.

Hopefully, it hadn't been tainted by my production at the bar last night.

# Chapter Four

N eeding a quick break from another busy morning of meeting with potential clients, I grabbed my steaming cinnamon dolce latte, a copy of the Bay Gazette, and sat at a little table tucked off to the side of Java & Lattes. The café was nearly empty, save for an older couple at the window side seats on the opposite side of the door. Crossing my legs, I turned to gaze out onto Main Street.

Cheshire Bay was rapidly growing on me, and it had only been a couple of days. The cozy storefront windows were all nicely decorated in a way that I couldn't help but go and check out. Even though I thought it borderline cliché, most had catchy little names, like Whimsical Whims, Hannah and her Scissors, and Daisy's Delights, all of which had signed contracts for the full twenty-two weeks. Things were definitely looking up. I wasn't going to be eating boxed mac and cheese this month.

I focused back on the Gazette, chuckling as I read the gossip section until I spotted Adam over by the till. How did he come in?

The unique doorbell chime installed as a pressure plate by the door hadn't activated, and I surely would've seen him walk right by me. My head tipped to the side as I worked out how he magically appeared.

"Deep in thought?" He sauntered over with his drink in hand.

I shook my head and tore my gaze away. Damn, the guy was stunning and probably put more effort into his looks than I did, which was saying something. "I was just wondering how you got in here."

"Back door. Joe lets me sneak in that way." He paused and studied me. "The back door of my shop is next door. It's quicker than walking around the corner."

"That makes sense." But somehow, I didn't feel satisfied with his answer.

"How's the move-in going?"

"All done. Chloe did most of it as she brought almost everything with her. I just brought the remainder." And unpacking that was relatively easy. Three-quarters of it went into my room, and the rest was scattered in the living area.

He rocked back and forth on his heels. "We're still on for our date tonight?"

I nodded and swallowed. "For disclosure, I'm agreeing as I think it's good business sense for me to see the area."

"Oh-kay." He drew the word out into two distinct syllables.

"You said it was a date, and I'm saying it's not; it's a business arrangement." My tone was clipped yet professional.

"A what?" He set his drink down on the table.

Fearing that I had somehow offended him, I backtracked a little. "A date, to me, leads one to believe it's of a romantic nature." I held my breath and stared at the undone top button of his shirt, waiting to see if further explanation was necessary. It was. "And in keeping with my full disclosure, I'm not in a place in my life where I'm ready to date or become romantically involved with anyone."

"You getting over a divorce?"

"It's not up for discussion. Sorry." My private life was just that – private. Only a very small handful of trusted people knew the truth, even if one had used it against me.

He rubbed his chin and reached for his drink, taking a long swig as he stared in my direction. "Fair enough." He paused and added, "You're just a one-night type?"

His brows had scrunched together, and I was worried I'd upset him, or worse, led him to believe in something that wasn't there. I needed to be upfront as I wasn't interested in any kind of relationship. Like never again. My only goal in moving to the area was to be my own boss. That was more important to me than dating or messy entanglements where others saw more than there was to see.

"Something like that." Mirroring his actions and hoping to calm the air between us, I too took a long sip of my drink and smiled. "I am looking forward to seeing what this area is all about, and I'm excited to have you as my tour guide. If you're still interested." I dangled the carrot almost hoping he would change his mind.

Pride stretched across his face, melting the tension like an ice cube in the sun. "The whole area is really a hidden gem."

"And everyone knows everyone else too?"

He looked at the section I tapped. "Ah, yes, the good ole gossip column."

"I've never read anything like this. It's not bad things at all. More like highlighting the good, like the comment about the mom and her two kids picking up garbage."

It was amazing to read all the little things mentioned, and truly, it couldn't be classified as gossip. I knew all about that and had been the target of it many times, and this wasn't it.

"It's great, isn't it? May I?" He pointed at the vacant chair across from me and dropped into it when I nodded, tipping his drink toward the window. "Something I love about this place. Yes, it's beautiful and tourists flock here in droves – you'll see come summer – but it's more than just being a seaside community. It's like we're all family and everyone tries to see the best in each other, and that's a beautiful thing."

"For real? I thought small towns were full of Nosy Nellies and everyone getting into other's business." I re-crossed my legs as I turned to face out the window and see it as Adam did.

"Oh, there are those too. Guess it all depends on how you look at it."

"And you see it as a glass half full?" I cocked an eyebrow.

Perhaps I'd become jaded from living the big-city life, although Victoria could hardly be called a big city, even if it was the capital of the province. It paled in comparative size to Vancouver, the metropolis across the strait.

"You don't?"

I shrugged, watching a couple walk hand in hand down the street. The dark-haired female opened the door for her blonde partner. "Still too new to make a judgement call, but I'm interested in seeing the reasons to give weight to one side or the other."

"Sounds like a challenge I can get behind."

Dammit, that smile of his was going to be my undoing. Maybe that was his plan.

He tapped the screen of his watch and jumped out of his seat. "Oh shoot, I need to go. See you at four?"

"I'll be ready."

"Wear comfy shoes."

Hmm... what did Adam have up his sleeve? Whatever it was, and despite my insistence that it was only a business *arrangement*, the butterflies took flight. What was I getting myself into?

# Chapter Five

I stood in front of the bathroom mirror, checking out my profile from every angle. Yes, it was just two small business owners getting together, but something about it being *him* had my heart pounding and my brain telling me to put in a little more effort but to also be cautious and make sure I was as transparent as hell.

I wasn't offering more than an acceptance of a tour of the area. That was all. It wasn't a date, and I didn't owe him anything. It wasn't even a business deal with strings.

My brush dusted a small finishing touch of powder across my forehead and nose. It was as good as it would get. After another glance at my dark, polished ponytail, I grabbed a zip-up hoodie from the front closet and drove over to the bookstore wearing my most comfy runners.

The bells chimed as I stepped inside the quaint little bookstore.

"Hey, Summer. Just give me a minute, and I'll be ready to

go."

"Don't rush. It's all good." I perused the local author section, unknown names with unique titles dancing across the display.

Picking up a book by BJ Sutcliff, I flipped it over and gave the back copy a read, adding it to my mental to-be-read pile. Suddenly, the ideas swirled. Would having a local author be a great thing for the market? Each week could be someone new, as surely there were at least twenty-two local authors who'd be willing to participate. It could be a revolving type of feature. As I counted the display of names, there were ten in view. Possibilities swirled inside my head while I tried to plan how it could work. I dug through my purse, grabbed my notebook, and jotted down the idea, along with the displayed names.

"Sorry for keeping you." Adam appeared from behind the counter. "Just finished up a text with my sister."

"Not a worry." I pointed at the local author's display. "How does this work?"

He shrugged, gave the back of his neck a rub, and doing so released a whiff of his exotic cologne. "For the most part, they approach me and ask if I'll carry their books. I take a small order, and if it sells out quickly, they'll bring in more. And if it doesn't sell in the allotted time frame, well, at least we tried."

"Hmm. Do you do events with them?" I set a book back onto the display, straightening it out.

"I wish. Sadly, there's just not the space in here for it."

The tightly confined bookstore didn't have the square

footage, however, my mind reeled with even more possibilities – like featuring a local author in the fair. But how to make it work?

"Hey, why don't you invite them to your market?"

"The thought has already crossed my mind." A smile bubbled out from the inside. "It could be a great idea."

"It's a damn good idea. I can provide contact names and websites for you."

I swallowed, wondering what that information would cost. "Thank you. That's helpful. What will I owe you for that?"

He gave me a long lingering, eyes narrowing stare. "Nothing. Consider it part of the service I provide as a tour provider."

"Nothing is free. There are always strings attached somewhere."

He cocked his head to the side. "No, I swear it's free." For a moment, he stared at me, eyes narrowed, and then shaking his head as if to free the thoughts, he walked behind the counter and pulled out a bag with the Barnes & Noble logo on it. "Before I forget, again, I have something for you."

I stared at his competitor's bag, speechless.

"Oh, that?" He pointed to the logo. "It's nothing. My ex loved shopping there when we'd go to Seattle as the books were a little cheaper." A tinge of sadness – or was it regret? – coated his words. "It was just a bag I had laying around."

"You kept the bag?" Of all the questions to leak from between my lips, that had to be the dumbest, and yet, probably the smartest. I had no right to probe into his personal life like the other inquisitive questions that threatened to vocalise first.

"It's a great bag; sturdy and reusable. And now it's yours." He pushed it closer.

I peered inside, and a rush of heat flooded across my chest and cheeks, staining them a brilliant crimson colour.

"The things you left behind." He shifted on his feet and thrust his hands deep into the pockets of his jeans. "On Saturday night."

My one-night stand. With the cowboy. My flats were in the bottom, the sparkles dim in the darkened space, with my bra and panties resting on top.

"They're washed by the way because it would be weird to return them as... Well..."

If a hole had opened in the floor and swallowed me whole, I'd be less surprised. I grabbed the bag, folded the top over, and tucked it under my arm.

As if he hadn't handed me the most embarrassing package, he asked casually, "Can get you to step outside for a minute, I just need to set the alarm."

I backed away, nodding like a bobblehead. "Oh, yeah, no problem. Front or back?"

"Depends. Are you okay if I drive? It's easier than giving directions, but if you're okay with me being your vocal map, I'm good with that too." He waited for my answer while he rocked on his heels, which upon further inspection, were not the cowboy boots he danced in.

"You know what, I prefer to drive." It was a control thing,

and I watched to see if it bothered Adam in the least. His gaze held me for a heartbeat longer than I expected, but there was zero issue of me being the driver.

Aside from the control factor, driving was the best way for me to learn where these places were. I'd be an active part in getting there since as a passenger, I had a learned ability to zone out.

"Fair enough." He pointed to the front door where I came in. "I'll meet you out there in two minutes."

I walked outside to my car and tossed my embarrassing bag of reminders into the trunk. Quickly I opened the passenger door and gave the front seat a quick dusting. It wasn't showroom ready, but it wasn't a pigsty either. I'd just closed the door when Adam came out the front.

"All good?" I asked.

"Locked up tight." He pulled the key out of the lock. "So, what would you prefer to see first? I can show you the local points of interest, or the different services and businesses here. You tell me what you'd like."

"Well... I think I'd like to see what hidden gems are around here."

"My kind of thinking."

I left his door open and slid behind the wheel. "Tell me the way."

Adam gave interesting instructions – a myriad mix of *at the big rock turn left onto Main Street* type. Following his easy directions, we arrived fifteen minutes later at a small strip of concrete parking markers, nestled at the base of a grove of trees. There'd been no clear roadway here once we turned off the main road; it almost felt like I was driving on private property.

"This is Glass Beach. Just park over there."

I stopped the car alongside a gravel road, near the open path Adam pointed out and the two of us clamoured out of the car. The area was deserted, although it was the end of March and a little cool for a dip in the ocean.

"Through here." He led the way down the well-worn path, pausing for a minute. "You've seen the main beach in Hardy Beach, correct?"

"Yeah."

It was your typical postcard perfection; a long strip of white sandy beach, ocean waves rolling effortlessly along the coast.

"This isn't like that at all. It's better."

Better? How could anything be better than that?

I pushed past him, stepping over an exposed root, and made my way to the ocean. As I cleared the trees, I stepped out onto a beach filled with colourful stones nestled against black sand. Beyond that, in what could only be described as a cove, was a beautiful stretch of sandy beach and in the water, pushing out against the surface were large, jagged rocks. How was this better than the picturesque beach near the airport?

To me, there was no surprise as to why it wasn't crowded.

"You're disappointed." Not a question, but 100% a statement.

"It's not that." But I didn't know the words to use that would erase the grey cloud shadowing Adam's face. "I've just never seen anything like this." For good measure, I bent down and scooped up a handful of the coloured rocks. "What is this?"

"Sea glass."

"Like actual glass?" I admired the frosty blues and greens in the palm of my hand and bent down to pick out an orange and white piece.

"Mostly. True sea glass comes from shipwrecks and broken bottles and tableware, tumbled and worn down until the edges are smooth and it gets this frosted appearance." He plucked a large blue piece from the assortment at his feet and held it between his finger and thumb for me to inspect.

Indeed, it was truly a magnificent shade of muted sky blue and admiration for this hidden gem washed over me like the gentle waves caressing the beach.

"It's lovely."

"Most pieces take a minimum of twenty years to become this, and some even as old as a couple hundred years."

I stared at the glass in my hands. Was any of this that old? "It's like holding time in my hand."

He chuckled. "Something like that, yeah. However, the true sea glass pieces are likely long gone." He stepped to the side as a slow-moving crab threatened to touch his boots. "The stuff you're holding, it's been made from garbage and has no value."

"Oh?" I stared at the pieces in my hand. Garbage or not, they were magnificent to look at.

I shoved the five different coloured pieces into my pocket.

"There are locals who scour the beaches every morning hunting for those rare treasures, and they make them into jewellery for the most part."

Those people I needed to locate. They would be an asset to the market, selling something truly unique and local to the area.

"But come out of the cove and over to the beach area. It's nicer." Adam led the way over the coloured glass rocks, and down to the main beach. "But don't look that way."

Of course, I had to look. "Why?"

"If you have trypophobia, I'd avoid going in there for a better look."

"What kind of fear is that?" It was a beach, filled with sea glass, sand, and trees. What could be frightening over by the logs and bush?

The Adam's apple bobbed, and he took a quick breath. "Some feel queasy when they see a bunch of clustered holes on something. And back that way, there are some items that have that."

I scanned the area, really hoping to see what this was all about. I'd never heard of such a thing, but I pulled out my notebook from my purse and wrote it down. "To ask Chloe."

He paled as he shrugged and turned away.

"Do those hole clusters bother you?"

"Immensely."

*Wow.*

Rather than explore the area to better understand what bothered him, I instead followed him over a giant log and set foot on the grainy yet sandy beach.

"It stretches each way for a half kilometer, and in the summer, you'd be hard-pressed to find a spot. Because it's not as accessible as Hardy Beach, or any of the main beaches really, the tourists don't visit, so it's pretty much full of locals."

I stared at the peaks of rock barely visible along the horizon and tried to imagine what the place looked like during a storm, with rolling fog. Likely had an element of something from a horror movie, and I couldn't wait for the first storm of the season to come and see it in action.

Adam carried on while I pictured the area darker and stormy than the overcast skies blanketing us. "If you are into whale watching, the grey whales tend to migrate through here."

"Are you serious?"

The firm expression on his face said as much. "Really? You didn't know that?"

"Nope. I figured that was on the other side of the island, through the strait."

"You really need an involved tour of the area." He looked down at me with a twinkle in his deep blue eyes. "Come on. We'll see if we can see any as they start heading south." Without asking, he grabbed my free hand and tugged me along.

Flashbacks. Anger. Fear. A memory flooded over me faster

than I could control. Being taken to a place I didn't want to go with someone I wasn't familiar with.

"Stop." I forced myself to plant myself back in the moment as my heart pounded incessantly and my breath came in short peaks.

Adam dropped my hand like a hot potato. "You okay?"

Centering myself as quickly as possible, lest he thought I needed a psychiatric assessment, I dug my feet firmly into the sand. "I'm fine."

"You're not. You've lost all your colour." He stepped closer but managed to keep a respectable distance.

I inhaled and formulated a lie. "I don't know how to swim, and if we should fall into the water, I'll drown."

Extreme? Yep. Way out there? Oh definitely, but it appeared like he bought it. Hesitantly, however.

"It's just an outcropping of rocks. Sure, it's a little slippery, but we'll be fine."

I kept my hands firmly at my sides, trying to betray my true reasoning, and to replant my walls as a rush of crimson-stained heat flooded my cheeks and chest; my Pinocchio-like tell. Closing my eyes briefly, I opened them to see him with a weary, yet concerned expression on his face.

"Fair enough, if you're that scared, it's an easy enough problem to avoid. We can always watch from the land. What about that hill?"

Off to the side was a small, climbable hill, more like a mound of dirt that had been neglected for years and started growing weeds.

Still, it was the perfect accompaniment to the lie.

"Looks ideal, thank you." I inhaled and kept a distance as my heart slowed to just enough to the speed limit.

"Your colour is coming back in spades."

Keeping my back to him, I climbed onto the nearest rock, and my toes dug into the soles of my shoes giving me a false sense of security, but I made it to the edge of a tiny embankment. It wasn't high up, maybe ten feet above the beach, but it did prove to have an encompassing view of the ocean.

Adam stopped beside me. "Harrison, that's my brother, he knows more about their patterns, but I think we may get lucky and see something. This is usually he time of year I think they migrate to the warmer southern waters."

Taking a cue from the direction of the endless ocean he faced, I too scanned the horizon, but I wasn't sure what I was looking for.

"There." He pointed out as his voice pitched.

"What? Where?"

He walked behind me and extended his hand in front of me. I ran my gaze down the length of his muscled arm, along his hand to the tip of his chewed fingernail. Beyond the tip, something, I can only assume a whale, jumped out of the water.

"Did you see it?" The frenzy in his voice was crystal clear, and his voice tickled my ear. It also caused a flurry of random butterflies to take flight.

I swallowed and tried to contain my excitement. I'd never seen a whale tail before, and it was much closer than I expected.

"That was… wow. Super cool."

"It really was. I didn't think I'd get so lucky."

Our eyes connected as he spoke, and I broke it by stepping back and away. "I'm going to grab a few pictures."

It was the stupidest thing to have said, but the moment needed an icebreaker, and if anyone could deliver a chilly reception, it would be me. I had a gold medal in it, thanks to recent events.

I took pictures of the beach and turned to take a picture of the ocean.

Adam stood on the edge, hands dangling beside him, a poster guy if ever there was one. He twisted his body in my direction.

"Do you mind if I take your picture?" I waved my phone.

He shook his head and resumed looking at the ocean while I held the button on my phone, capturing a dozen photos. Of him. Close up. From behind. Off to the side with the ocean sprawling to his right. In black and white, they'd be classic, and I couldn't wait to check them out when I was alone.

"Thanks." I pocketed my phone. "So, what's next on the must-see list? What could top this?"

"Are you hungry?"

My stomach growled at the thought. I'd only had a sandwich from the bakery for lunch. "Sure. What did you have in mind?"

"There's a little road-side place on the way to the tower."

"Tower?"

"You're not afraid of heights, are you?"

# Chapter Six

I wasn't sure why he asked me if I was afraid of heights until we arrived at the base of a steel tower that stretched infinitely high into the sky.

"It's decommissioned."

As if that made it any better.

A seven-story staircase, at least judging by the number of platforms and new sets of stairs, all lead up to a walk-around platform high above the ground. No doubt the view was out of this world. We'd already driven up the hillside that bore more resemblance to a mountain than a hill.

"Are you up for a climb? It'll make you even more hungry." He dangled the takeout bags steaming with a savoury scent.

"Let's go."

The climb was relatively easy, but still, we stopped at each level for a quick breath to take in the sight. Before we knew it, we'd climbed a hundred or more stairs and were at the top platform. The pointed part of the tower with a radio antenna went way above us.

Even though we paced ourselves on the ascent, the view from the center of the platform was enough to knock the wind of out me. The Pacific Ocean, in all her majestic grandeur, spanned the horizon, with a forest of treetops barely brushing the bottom of the platform. It felt like we were in the sky.

"Have a seat." Adam dropped onto the wooden floor and inched himself until his legs dangled over the edge without a care in the world.

"What are you doing?" My voice pitched while the skin pulled tight around my bulging eyes.

The only thing keeping him on the platform was a steel bar at armpit height. Hardly safe.

"I'm sitting?" He shot me a comical smirk.

I swallowed down a lump of raw terror. My fear of heights was a true, legitimate feeling. "But you're so close to the edge."

There was no way this was up to code, plus it had to have been highly illegal to be on the platform. Didn't we pass a sign that said no trespassing?

"Are you sure we should even be here?"

The air cooled, dropping at least ten degrees. It was enough to cause a violent shudder to ripple through me.

"You are afraid of heights, aren't you?"

"No." I glanced out to the ocean and inhaled a calming breath of pine-scented air. "Well, maybe. Yes. Yes, I am."

"I swear it's safe, and I have no reason to lie to you." He

gestured for me to sit.

Why wasn't there a bench nearby? The floor didn't seem practical. In fact, eating in my car was the best idea.

"It's all good." Adam patted a spot near him, but nowhere near the edge. "Trust me."

*Trust me.* Two words to incite a rush of adrenaline as they were often lies, said to invoke a false sense of security.

"I'm okay right here." Cautiously, stayed near the center of the platform. "Being eight feet away from the edge is close enough for me." I craned my neck and chanced a quick glance toward the platform's edge. It was all treetops and ocean, however, my stomach nearly revolted, and I hadn't even looked down. "My fear of heights only extends to when I'd look down on things... here, it's not..." I looked around. "It's not all *that* frightening." A sharp inhale of air expanded my lungs to capacity. "But to look over the ledge? No, thank you, Bob."

"Who's Bob?"

I shook my head and muttered, "It's just an expression."

He twisted around, leaving one leg dangling, and opened the bag. The aroma from the burgers and fries swirled around, making my stomach growl, and temporarily distracted me from staring at his disappearing leg dangling over the edge.

"Thanks for the food." He tipped a burger in my direction.

"It was the least I could do for my tour guide." I tried to send a cute wink his way, but my eyelashes got stuck together, and I had to pry them apart.

Rather than chew on the fact of me being a less-than-ideal dinner companion, I grabbed a burger, slowly unwrapping it just enough to keep a portion of it exposed.

Of course, the real reason for buying his dinner, and dipping into my meager savings, was I didn't want to be the unwilling recipient of a 'well, you owe me for dinner. Time to collect' motive. I'd had enough of that in Victoria.

Was Adam different? Who knew? I wasn't about to find out though as we weren't going to date. Yes, I banged him without knowing who he was, but that wasn't unusual, and amazingly enough, I was in complete control. Sure, the alcohol lowered my inhibitions and my walls, but I allowed it. And I could use a stiff drink right about now.

As I ate a bite, I watched Adam. Every so often, he'd look at me from the corner of his eye and then whip his head back to the sunset. For reasons I didn't understand, I was more fascinated with studying this guy, than absorbing the sunset filling the space around him.

"It's beautiful, isn't it?" He tipped his head to the ocean.

To the far left the sun dipped lower and golden rays wiggled across the horizon. Above me, the sky had turned a shade of lavender I'd never seen before. It was breathtaking how it melted and softened, changing into the orange ball hovering above the water. It wasn't painful to watch the sun either as a band of hazy clouds filtered it, making it easy to stare at and get lost within.

"Wow, that's something." There was a peace and calmness

finally settling around me, and those little niggles of worry dissipated as I shared space with Adam, who kept a safe distance, but also kept me firmly in his sights, but not in a threatening way.

Instead, I tore into my burger and had another bite, the crunchy lettuce puncturing the sound of silence.

After our burgers were done, he casually picked at his fries. "So, tell me, what brought you to Cheshire Bay if you have a fear of heights and water?"

I shrugged and swallowed. "A change really."

"From work?"

"From everything." I stared at the layers of bun, pickle, meat, cheese, and top bun. Slowly, I took another ladylike bite and chewed, trying to be quiet. "Actually, Chloe started the whole idea, after… Well, there came a time in our lives when she decided enough was enough. It was time for her to break away from her family's practice, and be her own boss, and after looking through some listings discovered a retiring doctor in a small town."

"Ah, yes, our beloved Dr. Singh."

"That's who it was." I snapped my fingers. "She mentioned how small towns are notorious for being passed over in favour of the big city life, but something about this place appealed to her. She accepted the job, dangled the carrot before me, if you will, and started planning her move. I was a bit of a chicken because even though I hated the people I worked for, I loved the job."

Mostly. Until things went too far.

"What were you doing?" The ice shifted in his cup after he

had a drink, and I jumped in surprise at the sound.

I tore my pulsating gaze away from his soda and pondered telling the truth about what I did previously. Propositions, side hustles, kickbacks; the kind of things that would get a person fired if the boss ever truly knew. However, the real job title was rather plain and unoffensive. "Event planning."

"Ah, that makes sense, based on your market start up." He grabbed a stack of fries and shoved a couple into his mouth.

"After some hesitancy and a bit of research into the area, I took the plunge, quit my job, and followed her. Now I'm my own boss, living by my own rules."

Walking away was one of the scariest situations I'd ever had to deal with, and I'd been a part of many unscrupulous encounters. Leaving the financial security, my great apartment, everything. But I had no choice in the matter as I was sinking, and fast, and now it was time for me to prove I could swim. Under my own banner and name, I needed to bust my ass and make sure I had enough business.

"Takes a lot of guts to do what you did. I can't imagine how hard it would be to leave everything behind."

He didn't know the whole story and if he did, he wouldn't be sitting here. Not with the likes of me.

I shrugged. "Thanks. Guess we'll see how the summer goes. Not sure yet what to do in the winter."

My big plan was the market, with hopefully a variety of other little events throughout. The winter still had a big question mark, but once I'd secured the minimums needed to sustain me over the summer, I was going to look into winter events. Surely there was a diverse assortment of festivals and such I could either tap into or set up.

I waved my hands through the air. "What about you? What's your story? Always lived here?"

"Only place I've ever called home."

"Wow, really?" I didn't mean to pose it the way it came out.

Adam twisted back around, dangling both feet over and wrapping his arms over the steel bar as well. Nervous butterflies swelled in my gut as he was way too close to the edge and with the sun dipping into the ocean, it was getting darker.

"Born and raised here. Never had any true desire to live elsewhere since everything I've ever needed was here. All my family and friends are here."

"They're all in Cheshire Bay?"

"Well, in the bay area. My older sister Erin lives near the edge of town, with my younger sister Francesca. I live downtown."

I laughed. Downtown had one main street and a few other roads that wrapped around. Hardly a downtown.

Adam continued despite my gentle chuckle. "My brother Harrison lives up in Stewart Surf; he's a whale watcher and works on one of the tour companies there, but we don't see each other much." There was a hint of hurt on the tip of his tongue. "And my best friend manages Birch Bay Burgers."

"Hey, Chloe and I had dinner there on Friday."

"Good food, eh?"

"Oh yeah." I glanced down at our garbage. "Tell me about your bookstore. That's a pretty interesting market to tap into in an eReader world."

"You'd think, right? But really, paper books are still selling strong, especially around here. You'll come to see how this area is more relaxed than the big city life you're used to." His inflections rose as he spoke with pride.

"I've already noticed. Not much is open in the evenings."

"That's true, but with all the scenery, there's still lots to do." A hearty laugh filled the air. "But I do keep the bookstore open one evening a week. It's slower, but that's the night I do my unboxings. There's just something about the way fresh books smell."

I smiled and playfully touched him, testing to see how my body would react. It was as electric as I remembered at the bar. "Unboxing? I think you need to find a hobby."

Although I wasn't one to talk. Event planning filled all my free time as there was always something I needed to take care of. Sixty-hour and seventy-hour weeks were not uncommon.

Adam finished off his fries. "Reading is my hobby. There are so many great places to escape into. I love how the authors craft this whole new world and readers become immersed in it."

"Is that where the name for the bookstore came from?"

He tipped his head back slightly, gazing into the heavens. "Could've been? But escaping into another world where time and space are different, well, there's just something amazing about that."

"Science fiction fan, are you?"

"Among others."

"Not romance though." I scoffed. Guys didn't read *bodice rippers,* an unfortunate reference to steamy reads, at least no guys I knew.

"While it's true romance is a traditionally female-dominated readership, of which 97 out of every 100 romance novels I sell are to woman, there are some guys who read it, and love it." He winked.

"That's curious. Are you one of the three percent?"

"It's like a little insight into the female psyche. Plus, I like seeing how women write men. Some are downright laughable, but others are bang on. At least guys who are more similar in nature to me. Being that I'm not a billionaire, or a rock star, or a hockey god sweeping the ladies off their feet, I can't speak on their behalf."

"That's why they're fiction. Real guys like that don't exist." I had, unfortunately, been introduced to a couple of millionaires who were not sweet and caring, and there was no sweeping a gal off her feet, not out of love and respect. I took in his languishing gaze on the sunset. "Did you always want to be a bookstore owner?"

In the distance, an owl hooted, and I flipped my focus to the treetops trying to spot the elusive hooter.

"Nah, sort of fell into it." His voice lost a bit of zest.

"How's that?"

He swung his legs like a child. "The owner got sick, and I started taking over for him, making the orders, and running the shop. When he died, I didn't have it in me to close it down, so I took over."

"Wow, that was incredible."

"Couldn't let Grandpa down." He tore his gaze away, and his shoulders rolled forward.

The air cooled as the sun dipped further into the ocean, and I zipped up my jacket. Tucking away the garbage, I inched a little closer to the edge, but not enough to dangle any body part over.

"Wow, a family business, that's pretty neat."

His armpits hung on the railing. "This is my favourite place to come and think as it's the highest point in the bay area. I come up here and talk to Grandpa, mostly about the store. I've often thought of packing it in and daring to branch out into something new and different, but after a long one-sided conversation, I decided the best place for me was to stay in Cheshire Bay and operate the store and make it everything he'd ever wanted."

"That's… well, it's pretty admirable." Instinctively, I reached out and touched his firm shoulder.

"I didn't do it to be admired, I did it because it was the right thing to do. Sometimes, a business decision affects more people than it looks." Adam turned and looked deep into my eyes as he quickly licked his lips.

And that was the cold, hard truth. One I knew all too well.

My heart fluttered, and instinctively I held my breath, holding in the moment while my gaze flittered from his eyes to his perfectly poised mouth and back up again.

Breaking the connection as fast as I could, I yanked my hand off his shoulder, chastising myself. I couldn't allow Adam to think this moment was leading anywhere. I needed to be resolute in my stance against any possible relationship development. Those were for others. Not me. Reliving the past wasn't in my future.

"Should we get going before it gets too dark?" I cleared my throat, rose, and grabbed the garbage. Best to leave before I made a giant ass out of myself.

"Yeah, sure. Everything okay?"

I glanced around into the hues of twilight and further zipped my hoodie while pacing around. "I'm just not a fan of the dark, and with no lights coming on, it's going to get really hard to see."

Another lie, but whatever, and thankfully in the encroaching darkness, he couldn't see the heat searing across my cheeks.

"Now that I've unwittingly discovered what you fear, you should tell me what you enjoy, so the next tour will be better."

"I don't know what I truly enjoy."

"For real?" We descended the first set of stairs.

I shrugged. "I've been so busy working, that I haven't yet discovered what I like doing in my spare time."

"Even as a kid or teenager?"

"Those were different times, and people change. I no longer play with Barbies, and I really enjoyed that."

He stopped and laughed. "True, but I think you like dancing."

A small smile seeped onto my face. "There is that."

We descended back to my car, the scraping of our shoes on the wooden staircase the only sound. That and the beating of my heart, something I was going to have to put the brakes on. Fast.

We drove in silence to the bookstore, where I parked in front.

"I figured I'd drop you off here, and then you could grab your car to go home."

He narrowed his eyes at me, cocking his head ever so to the right. "Don't you remember? I live above the store."

Dipping my head lower to see out the passenger window, I gazed up at the building. Oh. Well then. Shit. "To my defence, it was dark when I left."

"Were you possibly still drunk?"

"Very likely." The time ticked away with each beat of my heart. Awkward was my middle name. Nodding like an idiot, I begged my brain to come up with something. "Thanks for the mini tour. You were right, there are some truly amazing hidden gems around here."

He hesitated before he opened his door. "Would I be out of line if I invited you upstairs for a glass of wine?"

I held my breath. My body wanted to scream oh hell yes, and see where the night took us, but my brain jammed on the breaks so hard my head was spinning. Rather than speak, I shook my head.

"Did I do or say something wrong?"

"I didn't dare look him in the eyes.

"Does it have to do with me opening up? I thought women liked that sort of thing."

The little strings of lights stretched across the road waved in the breeze, swaying back and forth as they held my focus.

"I swear to God, it's not you, and it has everything to do with me, okay? I just can't. It's not for me."

"What's not for you?"

"Dating." I shook my head after I whispered the word. "Thanks again for the tour."

He sighed and exited the vehicle, hanging his head back in for a minute. "Oh, I forgot to mention. I'll be booking my weeks for the market tomorrow."

Slowly, I turned in his direction but stared at the collar of his polo shirt. "Thank you, I appreciate your business."

"I guess I'll see you around?"

"Yes, you will. I'll be in touch."

With a quick goodnight, he waved and closed the door, and I drove away. At least I hadn't totally wrecked the business deal and was going to have to work doubly hard at keeping my distance from the charming Adam Normandy. All it would lead to was total heartbreak. For both of us.

# Chapter Seven

J ava & Lattes was humming; customers lined up and took their drinks to go. Apparently, the unusual cold snap was responsible, and the residents were finding extra ways to keep warm.

I didn't blame them.

Sitting in the corner of the café, I sipped on my favourite drink – a maple macchiato – and focused on the spreadsheets and emails before me.

Finally, after two weeks of hard work, my first market was ready to open on the weekend, and I prayed the cold dissipated by then. I could only hope the weather forecast was correct in its prediction of hot, sunny weather.

Adding in the last of the details onto my spreadsheet, I reviewed the vendor list, pleased with the bookings. To make this sustainable, I needed a minimum of twenty vendors per week and as I recounted the list, I was well above that threshold, but my margins were tight – very tight. Too tight if I were being completely honest. In order to save on some of the costs, I was going to have to pull some strings. But where?

I didn't want to have to fall back to my old ways. And I promised myself, this time would be different.

"Every time I see you, you've got your laptop open."

Startled, my heart pounded as Adam's shadow covered my workspace. My gaze jumped to his handsome face – a day's worth of whiskers, and the lighthearted creases on the edges of his deep blue eyes.

"One might think you're a workaholic."

A smile I fought to control leaked out. "At my old job, sixty-hour weeks were the norm."

"That's insanity."

"That's the event marketing business." And didn't include the evenings wining and dining the clients.

I hit save on my worksheet. Last thing I needed was for it to disappear.

"How've you been?"

It had been two weeks since that night on the beach and at the tower, although it hadn't truly been the last I'd seen of him. Sometimes, he'd pop in to grab a coffee while I was working, and I pretended to be on the phone, casually peeking out of the corner of my eye to spy on him. Or I'd see him around town, and duck into the nearest store to avoid running into him face-to-face. Not that I really wanted to not see him because he was easy on the eyes and even easier to talk to, but those kinds of things never went well, and assumptions got made.

I took a sip of my sweet yet tasty drink and leaned back in my seat. "Aside from feeling under the weather, I've been good, you?"

"That's rough. Did you catch a cold?"

"Not sure. It could be just the stress of moving here and diving headfirst into starting my own business."

My anxiety levels were on par for some of my last events with my former company. High-profile clients meant scrutiny. Everything and anything was under a microscope. Back-room deals were made with a wink and a handshake, not like the contracts I had drawn up for each vendor. There were no hidden agendas – everything was clear. Crystal clear. Still, it picked at my soul, and I worried it wasn't as straightforward as it should be. Everybody wanted something that wasn't listed.

"I'm sure it'll go well."

I raised my hand and crossed my fingers. "Hope so."

"If it helps, I'm prepared and very excited." There was a glint in his eye, but it could've been the reflection of the overhead lights. "I even have a couple boxes ready to go."

"Excellent. Judging by the comments on my social media platforms, it sounds like quite a few people will check it out."

From previous experience, only twenty-two percent of people who click the *going* button actually did, but I was banking on other forms of traffic to show up and shower the vendors with visits and purchases.

"Did you manage any local authors?" He raked his hand through his thick hair.

"A few, yes."

He grabbed an empty chair and set it across from me. "May I?"

I nodded and held my breath. Maybe if I didn't breathe in his spicy scent, my roaring feelings would settle down.

"Would it be possible to know which authors and what weeks? I'd hate to put any of their books in my display if they're working the market that week."

"That makes sense." My gaze left his face, falling over his royal blue sweater, finally settling on my laptop. With a couple of quick clicks, I sent the list to him.

His phone pinged almost immediately, and he gave it a cursory glance. "Thanks. You're quick."

Adam drummed his fingers against his cup, slowly, pensively. He opened his mouth to speak and closed it, taking a sip of his drink. Finally, he blurted, "There's this regatta festival happening in Stewart Surf at the end of the month…" He paused and ran a finger over the lid of his drink, picking up a droplet of the creamy mixture before licking it off. "I was wondering if you'd like to go?" A quick gaze up into my eyes, where he held me. "Strictly as a business proposition."

I broke the focus and it landed on my computer. "How would that work?"

"Well, being how you're an event manager and all, figured

you could check out the competition and see about bringing something like that here. It doesn't have to be an epic event, but perhaps something fun to bring all the residents together. We already do a fantastic Christmas gathering on Christmas Eve, but it would be nice to have other events and festivals to go to."

"Really?" My mind started racing at the possibilities.

There were so many events my former company planned; from food truck nights in the neighbourhood to festivals to tailgate parties, depending on who was in charge of the event.

"Tell me more about this Christmas gathering?"

"We have three to four food trucks, a tree lighting, the skating rink is open with live music, and there are hayrides all around the area. It's a not-to-be-missed event."

"Sounds great." Something like that wouldn't be too hard to put together either. "And this event in Stewart Surf, what's it like?"

He shrugged. "Don't know, never been. Just happened to see the ad while I was flipping through social media and a friend grabbed me a couple of tickets."

"That's truly the way to go." Because as much as I hated it, word spread quickly that way, and algorithms were my new best friend. "This regatta, it would be strictly a business thing?"

"Just checking out the competition, but you know, we'd have to blend in." He wiggled his brow and a familiar tugging brewed in my chest, rendering me speechless. Thankfully, he carried on. "There's a dance, the docks are full of boats of all kinds, some of which you can tour. Plus, the boat house apparently has a live band.

It's a whole mini-festival. Having fun is their number one goal."

I laughed. "Sounds like you've done your homework."

He leaned in closer. "I'm a sucker for a good dance party, as are a lot of other folks. You have dancing at your event, or the possibility of it, you'll have a good turnout."

"But don't people flock to the two bars in town?"

He leaned back on the bistro-style chair, propping his leg atop his knee. "Amber's Ale is in the process of being sold or having the ownership transferred to a family member, who may or may not keep it running. Amber, the owner, she's engaged to a tycoon by the name Antonio Welch."

The name rang a bell, perhaps from the gossip column?

"The Cowboy Den is an utter dive, and everyone here knows it. I go there for cheap drinks and a lively, if not a little rowdy, atmosphere. Remember? There was a bar fight the night you and I were there."

How could I have forgotten? My cowboy hat wearing one-night stand contained a fist-flying dude who thought he was helping his buddy when in reality, nothing could've been further from the truth.

"At Christmas time, people break into dance around the ice rink and often sing along with the band. Oh, and carollers pop up en masse. It's truly something you'll have to see in December."

"This festival idea has some interesting ideas popping up in my head."

"Before you start planning your next event, how about an

answer? What about the regatta?" There was a borderline puppy-dog eye expression on his face, and if I didn't turn away and find something else to stare at, I was going to turn into a puddle of mush.

Instead, I swallowed and stared at the wrinkle forming between his eyes. "Umm, sure."

"Umm, sure?" His left eyebrow rose in a deep questioning way.

"That just feels more like a date thing to do."

"You're really hung up on not dating, aren't you?" Adam took a long sip of his drink, but he never removed his gaze from me.

"It's more than that. I'm just being upfront and completely transparent. That way, no one can read more into it than there is."

In a whispered hush, he muttered under his breath. "What did he do to you?"

"What?" My jaw unhinged and nearly hit the table.

"You're just so dead set against the idea of anything remotely looking like a date, I just wondered what your last boyfriend did to turn you against the very idea."

"Who said it was my last boyfriend?"

He studied me with a long lingering stare. "I read a lot, remember?" A hardened expression crossed his face, and a dark cloud hung over his head. "Well, I'm not going to get into specifics or anything, but when it comes to aggressive assholes, I know how that affects women. Long term."

I swallowed, hoping the hard lump would restart my dead heart when it plopped into my gut. It didn't sound like something he'd read, but something he personally had dealt with. There was a hard truth woven into his words, and a firm tongue as he added *long term.*

Rather than cater to whatever issues were casting shadows over my own disastrous mistakes, I felt an overwhelming need to deflect. "My lack of dating has everything to do with focusing on my career. That's not a bad thing."

"I never said it was."

"I'm at a point in my life where I just want the fun." I leaned closer so the rest of the café didn't hear. "Like the night of the bar. A no-strings type of thing."

"Ah, I see. No strings attached."

"Maybe Chloe is your…"

"Not my type." He answered before I'd even finished.

"Really?" Which threw me.

Chloe was everybody's type. Tall, hourglass figure, gorgeous blonde hair, and a smile that put you at ease, almost as if you'd fallen under a spell. And that's just her looks. Once you got to know her, she was everybody's best friend, a euphoric spirit with a bubbly personality. Probably part of the reason she was an excellent doctor – her bedside manner was incredible. I adored her more than she'd ever know.

"It is what it is." He shifted in his chair. "I need to get back to work, but the regatta, you're in?"

"I'm in." I nodded slowly as if to confirm and fought to hide the smile threatening to burst free.

He stood and pocketed his hand. "Perfect, we'll touch base and make arrangements later."

I watched him disappear into the back, my heart racing with each step.

It wasn't a date. Just two business acquaintances scoping out the competition. So why were the butterflies swirling about and my heart beating just a little faster at the thought?

# Chapter Eight

I t was the morning of my very first Bayside Market, and I was up with the sun, already on my third cup of coffee by the time I walked out the door. My stomach was a ball of knots, and I hoped everything went well. For all of us. The vendors weren't going to be happy if they weren't successful, and I wasn't going to rest until the last table left with a smile.

Bright-eyed and bushy-tailed, I arrived at the parking lot three hours before the vendors were due and met with the rental company providing me with twenty-seven tables and chairs.

"How do you want them set up?"

"Oh, you provide that? I suspected you were just dropping everything and taking off."

"It's extra, but you don't look the type to do this on your own." He pumped his burly biceps for good measure. "Slip me a fifty, and this'll all be done within thirty minutes."

I didn't have the extra money to spare, and besides, as I

looked into the back of the truck, it shouldn't be too hard. I'd start at the far back of the parking lot and work my way to the front. Labour intensive, but definitely not impossible.

"It doesn't have to be cash." He stood there with an expression on his face I was all too familiar with.

Not this time. I promised. I was in control. "I'll be good, thanks. Plus, my help will be here shortly."

He shook his head and muttered "women" under his breath. He unloaded the first cart of tables. "The carts are included, but any damage, and you'll pay for them."

The hairs stood up on the back of my neck, suddenly terrified I was going to have a list of surplus charges.

While he unloaded the second and third carts, I grunted and pushed the first ten tables to the far end of the lot. Unfolding my layout with precise measurements, I gave it a glance, and walked back to the delivery truck.

"Did you need tents?"

"Not today, thanks."

The weather was going to be perfect, warm but overcast. However, I would budget it in for the hot summer dates to keep my vendors out of the direct heat.

He unloaded a cart of folding chairs and parked it beside the two carts of tables. "I'll be back at four-thirty for pick up."

"Perfect, thanks."

Attached to the clipboard was a business card. Just a first name and phone number. "If you want a sweet deal on things, call me directly. These are mine, and I can give you a better price than the rental company."

I fought the shudder but pocketed the business card as I scrolled through the clipboard, rereading it over to make sure nothing additional had been added, and once satisfied, I signed it.

The festival ran until four, but maybe if I asked nicely, the vendors would fold up their tables and place them on the cart. Would that be asking too much?

"Good luck, lady."

I pushed the second cart into the middle of the parking lot as the diesel truck roared to life and left me alone.

Two sweaty hours later, I had the tables and chairs set up in a long U formation. Thank goodness I'd given myself the extra time.

I'd just posted taped numbers on each of the tables when the first gung-ho vendors started arriving and a flurry of excitement filled the air as vehicles unloaded, introductions were made, and tables became decorated. It filled my heart with joy.

After setting up the cheap-looking sandwich boards on the road, I stood at the entrance to the market, while the last of the vendors decorated their space. Gazing down the line of tables, I worried there wasn't enough of a grand display, and perhaps adding the tents as a weekly setup would help give it more of a market feel. I felt for the card in my pocket wondering what the cost would be, knowing it was something for a future date. Today had to do as it was.

Hanging my head that it wasn't as perfect as I'd hoped, I set up the two eight-by-eight banners on the edge of the market entrance, angled just perfectly to lead the buyers in. Each banner had the new and expensive Bayside Market logo. It cost me the week's worth of vendors to get it made pushing me further into the red with a screaming credit card balance, but it was worth it. I couldn't help but smile. Deep down, there was a sense of pride as I glanced at my first major event. I'd done it on my own. *All* on my own. No dirty deals needed.

"Looks good." His voice was as smooth as butterscotch, and I twisted to look up into his face. "Coffee?"

I took it from his hand, not knowing until that moment how parched I'd become. "Thank you, Adam, your timing on this was perfect."

"Figured you might've been run off your feet." He rested his forearm on top of a dolly stacked with boxes of books and scanned the crowd of people putting the last-minute touches on their displays. "I think it'll be a great day."

I gave the fading grey skies a once over. "Sounds promising. Weather's looking good."

A reminder went off on my phone. Fifteen minutes until we officially opened, but judging by the cars coming down the lane, we were going to have some early birds.

"You should go and get set up. I know I have a few more things to finalize before we officially start letting the buyers in." My focus hopped from table to table and behind me to the parking lot. "I'll come by and chat in a bit."

"Absolutely. Good luck."

"And to you." I wanted this to go well. I needed it to prove I wasn't a failure.

Heading over to the first vendor, I snapped a picture of their setup. One by one, I was uploading them to the website and all my social media channels, in the hopes that if people saw what was being offered, they'd make the drive down.

A couple of hours into the market, and the place was packed. It floored all my expectations and hopes. Everywhere I looked there were thick throngs of people, and hopefully, for my vendor's sake, they were of the buying variety, although judging by the bags on the arms, it was safe to assume as much. I wandered past the tables, making my way over to Adam's, curious to see how the bookshop was doing. I shouldn't have wondered; his display stand had a new set of books, and a customer was flipping through them.

I moved beyond and stopped at Sylvia's Bakery. Sylvia, owner and baker extraordinaire, was unable to attend but sent a replacement. Libby had the energy of the Energiser Bunny and may have been on a sugar high as she was bouncing from side to side, greeting each customer with a large, infectious grin. Her display case was nearly empty.

"How's it going?" I had wanted to try one of the cinnamon buns, but they were all sold out.

"Great." She beamed enthusiastically. "I have one of my co-workers en route to bring more goodies. We're selling out."

"That's fabulous."

Another customer pushed in front of me and ordered some pastries.

"Libby's hard to say no to. She's got the best salesman skills, guess that's why she's always busy."

I flipped my gaze over to the wood carver who'd just spoken. "Erin, right?"

She nodded. "That's correct."

I stepped over to her display since a couple more people were placing orders with Libby. "How's things going here?"

Erin set her carving tool down and blew shavings off the bear she was working on. "I can't complain. Made a few sales so it helps pay for the day, plus I've had lots of inquiries."

"That's fantastic."

She wiped her hands on her apron and took a swig from her water bottle. "Thanks for setting this up. I'm not a marketer, so I've always struggled to get the word out, so if nothing else, I'm happy to have met a bunch of new and interesting people."

"Hopefully things will continue to get better with each sale. Sometimes it takes a bit to start building momentum."

"Adam said you have loads of experience with these kinds of things."

"Adam? The bookshop guy?" I quickly flipped my gaze in his direction where he was talking with an older gentleman.

Adam connected with me, and an easy smile popped onto his

face while he nodded at whatever the other guy was saying. The heat spreading to my cheeks was uncontrollable.

Erin cleared her throat. "That's my brother."

"Oh, really? Wow." He'd kept the lid on that pretty much sealed. "He's a nice guy, and he knows his clientele."

She leaned over her table and waved me closer.

I tipped my ear toward her.

"If you hurt him, in any way, shape or form, I'll return it tenfold. He's been through enough."

My words tripped over themselves, unsure of where her sudden hostility came from. "What? I'd never. I mean, we're not even..."

"I know about your one-night stand and the way you're now playing hard to get. Adam doesn't do one-night stands, so watch it."

I held my breath and tried to act like I wasn't bothered, but deep down I was downright terrified of how much she knew.

She kept her tone even and low. "You're the new flavour in town, and everyone knows it, my brother included. Don't toy with his heart, especially if you simply have an itch to scratch."

Rather than utter another word, I pulled my shoulders back and stood straight, avoiding even a slight turn in Adam's direction. Keeping my gaze focused on Erin's artwork, I gave her a quiet nod and stepped over to the next table.

I swallowed a morsel of fear and worried about what Erin was capable of because I knew from firsthand experience one didn't need to be built like a bouncer to inflict damage. Words were truly mightier than the sword.

I kept visiting with each of my vendors, but try as I did, I couldn't help stealing a casual glance first to Erin and then allowing it to float over to Adam, always through the corner of my eye.

Hurting guys, especially a sweetheart like Adam, wasn't on my business plan. No one was playing hard to get. It wasn't an act. I *was* hard to get to. Personal damages tended to do that to a person.

# Chapter Nine

The bass was pulsating and rumbling my car as Chloe and I grabbed the last available parking space at the Cowboy Den. There were ten-gallon hats and baseball caps as far as the eyes could see, along with the massive belt-buckles reflecting the white streetlights, it made it seem like I was on the coast with dozens of mini lighthouses.

"Should be some good pickings tonight." Chloe lowered the visor and rolled her gloss over her perfectly pouty lips.

"Well, there'll be guys, but I don't know about *good pickings.*"

"You're not choosy, it shouldn't be tough." She smacked her lips together. "Oh, which of us is the wingman?"

Which was also the designated driver. I lifted my fist. "One. Two. Three."

Chloe threw a rock, I threw paper.

"Guess that's me."

She lost last time too, and I felt a little bad for her. "You know what? I don't feel like getting drunk tonight. Why don't I be your wingman?"

"Nah, I lost fair and square. Besides, I could see these guys in my exam room and that would make things awkward."

"So next week we should go to another town then. Right?" I fluffed my hair and then pressed my breasts together to plump them up. "Get you some fresh blood."

"Fresh blood would be great." Her face lit up as she wiggled her brows. Suddenly, she narrowed her eyes. "Wait a sec. Isn't that Adam?"

Dressed like Chuck Norris in a blue denim shirt and blue jeans, with a tan cowboy hat, Adam, the meek and charismatic bookshop owner – strutted over to a group of similarly dressed guys.

"That's him. Different, right?" I pretended to root through my purse but kept my eye on him.

He had to be surrounded by buddies as there was a lot of back-clapping and nudging, especially as the ladies walked by.

"Well, let's go. You can stop by and say hi." Chloe put her hand on the door.

"I'll say hi, but that's about it."

She twisted her chest to face me. "What would be so wrong with having more than a one-night with him? He seems nice."

"You originally said he was boring."

"That's what makes him nice."

I rolled my eyes but kept my focus on the group of men. "Nice and boring is not what I'm looking for."

She sighed and pointed at a buff guy leaning on the hood of a car smoking a cigarette. "Him?"

The bad boy look had potential, but all I wanted was a good romp in the sack. Same as Chloe, although if the right opportunity presented itself to her, she'd be willing to go for a longer term.

"Maybe." I shrugged but tore my focus from the bad boy. With a mind of its own, it settled over Adam, watching as he shifted on his boots and wiggled his hips to the beat.

"Let's party."

We exited the car, and I smoothed out the crease in my pants. I was on the prowl and selected my wardrobe accordingly. Black heels and pleather pants, as real leather was way beyond my budget, and a light, flowery blouse. My hair was loose, but my makeup was on point – smoky eyes with wingtip liner. A glance in the mirror and I almost didn't recognize myself.

We made our way to the main door, right past Adam and his friends, pretending to not have noticed who they were.

One of the guys catcalled, and another whistled.

Chloe wiggled a little in response.

A deep voice, who sounded like Adam, but I didn't turn to verify, told the guys to knock it off.

Once we were through the heavy wooden doors, the honky-tonk music I wanted to get lost in consumed my soul. It was too loud to yell at Chloe and tell her I needed a drink, so I tapped her on the shoulder and made a drinking motion. She nodded and followed me through the sweat-soaked crowd to the long, polished brass railing bar.

I lifted my hand, splaying two fingers, and pointed at the long necks beside me. The bartender grabbed two beers and slid them my way. Passing one to Chloe we clanked the necks together, and I tipped back the cold, bitter ale, keeping a thumb over the mouth of the bottle.

My attention wandered, crossing over to the faces of the guys who turned to check me out. Guys tipped down their cowboy hats, and another gave me a shy smile, but most of them were young bucks. Too young for me, and I doubted they were of legal age – likely had fake IDs, like I had at their age.

We circled the dance floor – a giant pit sunken in the middle of the joint – and found a vacant table to rest our drinks on. As I took another long pull on the drink, I spotted a good-looking older guy prowling as he slithered through the crowd, eyes locked on his target; me.

"Wanna dance, pretty lady?" He yelled in my ear.

I nodded and passed my drink to Chloe before I followed him down onto the floor. In my heels I was much taller, but that didn't stop him from being one of the better dancers I've danced with, however, he wasn't swift enough to prevent injury. I actually slid into him once, and I hit my forehead on the brim of his hat.

He spun me around, his hand firm on my hips, and as we both faced in the same direction, I backed into him, grinding hard. He reciprocated and held on tight. Oh yeah, this guy would be easy to take home and ride. Ready to see how far we could push things on the dance floor, I squeezed my biceps together to push up my rack, something he was staring at intently. I tipped my head back to elongate my neck and while twisting my face, I spotted Adam dancing with Chloe, and Adam was carefully watching me.

It shouldn't have mattered, but it gave me pause, and suddenly I felt raw and exposed and naked. I righted myself and blinked. My dancing partner was not impressed with the change in my tempo and spun me around, but as I was unprepared, I ended up missing his hand and slamming it against his firm chest.

"Oh, hello," his lips mouthed.

He caught my almost-fall, wrapping his hands around my back, and slowly manoeuvring his grabby hands to cup my ass.

I put my hand against his chest, firmly, and pushed away. "Not tonight, asshole."

The moment was over. He'd taken without having asked first. My desire for this guy bounced away with each beat of the music, and I no longer wanted what he was so willing to offer. I was still in control – I called the shots.

I stormed back to our table and watched as the nameless asshole I'd just dismissed pulled Chloe into a line dance. She nodded to me, a tell that she was okay with this guy, so I remained steadfast in my spot where I could easily keep an eye on her. However, the way they tangled together on the next song – a slow melody – I had a feeling he'd be a breakfast guest. Chloe had found her entertainment for the evening.

My beer had been left unattended, but I was thirsty. Small towns weren't filled with the kind of guys who'd drop something into a drink, were they? Parched, I reached for my half-empty beer and gave it a sniff, followed by a light sip. Everything tasted okay, but not wanting to chance it anymore, I slammed it down on the table before another taste could tempt my tastebuds.

About to go and order another, one presented itself. From Adam. I accepted it eagerly and chased away the dryness in my mouth by guzzling over half.

A light burp erupted, but under the boot-stomping and music blaring, even I didn't hear it, and I was sure neither had Adam.

He tipped his head and finger gunned to the pit. "Want to dance?"

I did, I really, really did. Adam and I had a good time last time – a natural rhythm. I lifted a single finger to indicate one minute, and I polished off the rest of the bottle. Part of the reason I got so wasted last time was because it was a standard rule of thumb to not leave the drink unattended, and the best way to not have that problem was to finish it off before I left it behind. Slamming the bottle down and feeling the effects already, as it had been hours since I'd eaten, I led Adam out onto the dance floor.

For the next few songs, we lined danced and two stepped and cut loose. I hooted and hollered to the music and laughed until my stomach hurt. It was great to unwind and allow to the beats to fill my soul with each bar of music. This was my happy place. On the dance floor, I wasn't an event coordinator, and he wasn't a soft-spoken bookworm – we were both free to be the wild versions of ourselves.

A slow song came on, and I bowed to Adam in thanks and started to walk away. I didn't make it two steps before he tapped my shoulder, a questioning gaze requesting approval on his face.

What was the harm?

Like an awkward high schooler, I looped my arms around his neck, and we swayed to the *Keeper of the Stars*. With his hands on my hips, we rocked back and forth, the warm scent of his cologne filling my senses along with the light smell of beer on his breath. I leaned back a little to look at his face, and he stared down at me. His gaze travelled between my eyes and lowered to my lips before returning. He tipped his head to the side and slowly moved in closer.

I pulled back, shaking my head. I just wanted a dance. Or two. Or five. And yes, I enjoyed every minute with Adam, but I couldn't kiss him.

"I can't. I'm sorry."

Sex was sex. It meant nothing and happened so regularly, I no longer had any attachment to the activity. It was what it was – a means to an end.

But kissing? That was a whole other playing field. It was personal, and it had meaning. And Adam should've known that. Even our one-night stand didn't involve kissing.

It had been over seven years since I'd last kissed a guy.

# Chapter Ten

voiding Adam at all costs had become my new mission. If I wasn't around the guy, then there would be no way to hurt him. Mission accomplished, right? Except in a small town, avoidance was mission impossible.

Since Java & Lattes was next door to Adam's bookshop, I skipped out on working there and headed down the street to Sylvia's Bakery. The coffee wasn't as good, but the pastries were to die for. I'd have to do laps around the town to burn off one chocolate braid.

"Good morning, Libby." I strode up to the counter.

"Morning, Summer." She wiped a stray blond wave off her face. "What can I get you?"

"A regular coffee and–" I stared into the display case. "Oh, what the heck, I'll take one of the specials."

Her face lit up, and she plated an apple danish with vanilla bean icing. "Sylvia let me make these myself, so I hope it's yummy. If it's a hit, Sylvia says we'll add it to the menu. Here's a quick survey for when you're done, if you don't mind."

She put the plate, the survey, and a steaming cup of coffee onto a small tray.

"If it tastes half as good as it looks, it'll be a winner." I tapped my debit card against the machine after she rang up my total.

"Refills are on the house."

"Thanks." I grabbed the tray and walked over to where I'd set my laptop by the window.

Main Street was too eclectic to sit tucked away from it, and I was happy to have it as a distraction. I could people watch from the best seat in the place as they stopped to talk to one another. Everyone truly seemed to know the other. Mind-boggling.

After I got everything up and running, and logged in, I took a sip of the coffee and quickly set it back down. It tasted as if twice the amount of grounds had been added to the filter. I stifled a blech face. There weren't enough enhancements to make it palatable, but I was going to try. Foolishly, I added three packs of sugar and two tumblers of cream before I tasted it again. It was an improvement, but not ideal. I already missed the coffee from Java & Lattes. Sylvia's Bakery may have the market on pastries, but Java & Lattes had it for great, strong coffee.

I read through the anonymous comments from the vendors, since I had them fill out an online form about what worked and what didn't, and thankfully most of the feedback was quite favourable. Some had some great ideas, and some had far-out demands – things I just couldn't afford to provide, unless they wanted their low fees to be sky-high. Maybe, in the big city and in an indoor facility, but definitely not on a grassy strip in the Bay area.

I also scoured a couple of vendor requests I needed to research first to see if they were a good fit. I didn't just want to take someone's money for the rental and have their sale be a dud, I wanted them to be a success. Plus, they had to offer something unique and attractive.

I was just pulling up the website of a whale-watching tour a vendor had inquired about when my best friend burst through the door.

"Hey, Chloe." I waved from my seat.

She waltzed over in runners, jeans, and a nice silky top, and plopped down in the seat across from me. "Hey. Just picking up some staff room goodies. I'm interviewing today and trying to sweeten the pot."

"That's awesome."

Dr. Singh's receptionist had agreed to stay on, temporarily, until a replacement was found. She wanted to retire since her husband had just recently retired, but with a lack of resumes and applicants, Chloe had been afraid her receptionist was years away from retirement.

"Interviewing three." She grimaced. "Fingers crossed one of them will be perfect."

"You can only hope."

Her eyebrows crept toward her hairline and a sly smile stretched from ear to ear. "One of them is a young buck, wanting part-time work."

"Part-time? I thought you wanted full-time?"

"Beggars can't be choosers, and if he's cute, well, I can find a way to make it work."

"You can't date your employees. Isn't that against the rules?"

"Not against mine."

Of course, it wasn't.

Chloe just wanted a little fun and she wasn't picky who it was with. Case in point, the nameless cowboy from the other night turned out to have a name – Billy. But he didn't join us for breakfast. Apparently, as he rounded third base, they both realised they'd met each other before – he'd been with his pregnant girlfriend at the clinic.

"I think you need to read the code of conduct book again and see the bigger picture."

"Yeah, yeah, yeah." She rolled her eyes. "He looks good on paper though."

Libby waved and called out her name. "Dr. Tarkin, your order's ready."

She glanced at her watch. "Shit, I need to go. First interview is in twenty minutes." She grabbed the box off the counter and lifted it to peek inside. "These look even better than the website. Not sure if there'll be any for the interviews."

Ha-ha, a two-note chuckle sounded out of me. Chloe had the world's sweetest tooth which she fought against constantly. However, her workout schedule was impressive, and since she'd lost forty pounds a few years back, she'd worked hard to never gain it back. I envied her dedication. No doubt the piece of heavenly sin on my plate was going to add five pounds to my frame before I'd even leave the store, and I was already on the puffy side.

"Oh, for our dinner tonight?" She stopped in front of the door. "Let's go to check out someplace in Spirit Bay."

A little town thirty minutes away, apparently with the best view of the Pacific, at least according to the Frommer's Guidebook. Maybe not quite as good as the tower Adam had taken me to, but I was willing to check it out.

"Sure, that would be great." I nodded and wagged my finger at her. "Good luck. Keep your distance and behave."

"I don't know the meaning of either of those things." She laughed and blindly bumped into the man walking into the bakery. "Oh, hey, Adam."

"Oh shit." I dropped my gaze to my computer screen, pretending to be fascinated by the email staring at me all the while stealing quick glances at the confrontation.

"Dr. Tarkin," Adam said politely and held the door open for her.

With a quick wave, she ducked under his arm and disappeared.

"Ah, the workaholic." He sauntered over with a laugh on the tip of his tongue and stood a couple of feet away.

Fresh and clean, with a hint of the same cologne he'd sported on Saturday night, he looked damn good in his dark jeans and cable knit sweater. So different than the cowboy look. Both were appealing in their own, unique ways.

I took a sip of my awful coffee and stifled a grimace. Having purposely picked this location over the one next door to his shop, I'd hoped to avoid him, and yet, it was like the universe was laughing.

"Morning, Adam."

"Can I join you while I wait for my food?"

"I, umm, sure." I moved my laptop to the side and cleared a space at the round table for him.

He walked over to Libby and placed his order, returning in a heartbeat. "Did the market do well for you?"

Relieved how the first words out of his mouth were business related, I sighed and forced a breezy smile to tease my lips. I hadn't broken even, not even close, and judging by the spreadsheet, it was going to take a few weeks to do that. My fingers were crossed that by summer, I was going to start turning a profit.

However, I needed the focus away from me. "I should be asking you that."

He snickered and sat in the wooden bistro-style chair, leaning back casually, and clasping his hands behind his head. "Yeah, the store did well. Parker manned the bookstore while I was at the market, and together we nearly doubled our daily sales. I'm very happy."

"Fantastic." I tried to keep my tone light.

He avoided eye contact. "What about you? Was it successful?"

"All the vendors seem very pleased, so that makes me happy. I have additional vendor requests flowing into my inbox, and the comments on the pages are positive, so I'd say yes, it was successful. I'm going to be uber busy trying to make everyone happy."

"I told my friend Landon, as well as Harrison, about your market, so one of them may apply. Landon's a whale watching tour operator and truly caters a marvelous experience to the visitors."

"Actually, I recall seeing a tour company in my inbox."

"Landon's good people. Takes pride in his work and makes sure the customers are satisfied." He moved forward and tapped the stack of papers beside my computer.

"Sounds like a ringing endorsement. I'll give him a serious look over."

Adam finally locked his gaze with mine, and my heart jump-started back to life. Too bad it was my mind, and logic, and purpose, that took over, causing me to turn away.

As I watched people walk down the street, hand in hand, I kept a side eye on Adam. He was staring out the window, almost as if he was lost in thought. His left eye kept twitching though.

"Adam, order's ready."

"That's my cue." He stood and rocked back and forth on his feet as he jammed his hands into his pockets. "Umm, can I inquire about Saturday night?"

I held my breath and focused on the rivets of his jacket. The air between us already had the tension and pressure of an upcoming storm, something I desperately wanted to avoid, so I offered up a quick thought. "I had a good time dancing. You're a great dancer."

"Um, thanks, you too." He continued to rock on his heels, but no words ventured free. Finally, after a miserable few seconds, he blurted, "Do you have plans tonight?"

I swallowed and grimaced. "Chloe and I are heading to Spirit Bay for dinner."

"Oh, well. Okay." He raked his hand through his hair. One set of strands stood ramrod straight and refused to fall back effortlessly into place like the others. It was charming, much like the guy it belonged to. "While you're there, you should check out Castaways. They have a great selection of some real treasures, and if you're not too full, at the back of the place is an ice cream shop – very turn of the century kind – and they have the best rum raisin ever."

"Ever?" I could only hope he'd hear the playfulness in my inflections.

"Once you try it, you'll never buy the chain brands again."

I nodded and scratched down his suggestion into my notebook. "I can't wait."

"There's also this great hike, but it's not really a hard hike, just a little muddy, and it takes you up and over a local beach. It has a terrific view, but the light on the path darkens deceptively quick, so see it before the sun starts setting."

"How about I save that for another day? Chloe's not a big fan of mud, and we're going for a special dinner, so there'll be no time to clean up."

He laughed as he scuffed his runner over the floor. "I can see that about her."

"Maybe you can take me? One day?" The words fell out before I could stop them. *Why Summer? Why?* Hadn't I learned anything from Declan?

"Sounds like a date." His eyes popped open, and he tripped over his own vocalized thoughts. "I mean a plan. A plan. Good grief, I know you're not into dating. Or kissing for that matter."

I wasn't about to apologize for either.

Kissing was personal, and well, it had been a long time since I'd kissed anyone who meant anything important. Went hand in hand with the whole lack of dating aspect, although the reasons for that were longer than my vendor lists. It's who I was, and who I'd become, and that was never going to change. Not even for a guy as sweet as Adam.

# Chapter Eleven

Chloe flipped through the clothing in the far corner of Castaways, taking an item off the metal rack and holding it against her chest.

I shook my head. The mid-thigh crocheted sweater didn't match her colouring, or her style, try as she may to adopt the bohemian chic she thought was all the rage; it wasn't a look she could pull off.

"So, are you going to tell me about your interviews or am I going to have to guess?" Nestled between two knitted pieces, I spied a gorgeous sapphire sweater and held it up for her.

She stuck her finger into her mouth and mocked gagged. "Not for me, thanks, but you know what? It would look great on you."

I draped the soft yarn creation over my chest and turned to check it out in the full-length mirror hanging on the pillar. It looked homemade, as the label read *Grandma's Den,* but the deep blue crocheted pattern would look great over a silky tank.

I viewed the price tag. Damn, too expensive. Mind you, tonight's dinner was going to stretch out my meager pennies, but that's what credit cards were for, right? As long as the minimum payments were made each month, I was good until the money started flowing in.

Holding the sweater against my chest, I stared longingly into the mirror again.

"Are you going to get it?" Chloe asked as she stood beside me.

"Nah. I don't think it'll work with what I've got."

"It looks great on you though." Chloe continued to flip, the metal scratching against metal hurting my ears with each swipe of the hanger as she moved from clustered rack to rack.

Defeated, I hung the sweater back up.

"There's nothing here. Why isn't there something? In a store full of clothing, why can't I find anything that works?"

Although there was some of her metropolitan look in the store, anything brand new was mostly non-factory made or mass produced for the tourists with graphics that screamed tacky gifts. Not appropriate for the town doctor with her *finally settled in and belonging* look she thought she needed.

Leaving Castaways empty-handed, we headed out onto the boardwalk, right into the heat of the blazing sun. The spring sunshine warmed my soul.

"Tell me about your interviews. Why are you being so quiet about it?" I elbow-nudged her.

She kept walking and casually mumbling the names of the stores.

The lightbulb went off. "Chloe? Tell me you didn't hire the cute guy?"

She shrugged but didn't face me.

"You didn't?"

Stopping in front of a small set of stairs that led to the roadway, she planted a hand on her hip. "The other two were absolute garbage, and well… Justin's fresh out of college looking for a job and was willing to go full time when I offered him a little perk."

"Do I even want to know what that was?"

Her heels clicked on the boardwalk as she resumed her window shopping. "There it is." She sauntered towards the restaurant at the far end of the strip. "I know he's only temporary, but Darla wants to retire. This way she'll train him to replace her, he has a job, I have some eye candy, and everyone's happy."

I pulled her to a stop and stepped off the side as a mom with a double-wide stroller passed by.

Keeping my voice in check so as to not draw attention to us, I narrowed the distance between us. "You can't screw your new hire."

"Not even a little bit?" There was a pleading in her voice.

"Not even in your dreams. It's an imbalance of power, and you could come out looking bad."

"But his body." Her shoulders rolled inward, and her bottom lip curled out.

She took a few more steps and opened the door of D&W, the restaurant she'd wanted to visit. The names of places in Spirit Bay weren't as kitschy as Cheshire Bay, which was odd seeing as how Spirit Bay was more of a tourist trap. Maybe that was all part of Cheshire Bay's unique charm.

We walked into the modern-style restaurant where, after checking our reservation, the hostess escorted us to the far end of the place banked with floor-to-ceiling windows, lending itself to a gorgeous ocean-side view. She set down our menus on the linen placemats and stood expectantly.

Instantly, we both ordered a glass of red wine; I opted for the cheaper house while Chloe went for a better label.

"Okay, the view is great." I nodded, watching the dark blue waves roll along the sandy coastline as the gentle breeze ruffled the knee-high reeds of yellow-green grass.

"Right?" She sighed and linked her hands together, staring out at the surf.

A buff guy sauntered out onto the beach. It was a little cold to be wearing shorts, so I chalked him up to being a tourist from way up north because at 15°C, it certainly wasn't ocean-dipping weather.

"God, I need a man. Especially one like that." Chloe's face took on a dream-like quality.

"You don't."

"Oh, yes I do. I need to feel complete."

I folded my hands and set them on top of the leather-bound menu. "A man won't do that, and you and I both know it to be true.

Compliment you, sure, the right guy will do that in spades, but you're already complete. The whole two pieces of a puzzle coming together, that's – metaphorical."

She shook her head, and the sigh breathed out of her was a pitiful one. Her self-esteem had somehow taken a hit today. A little bit of poking, and she'd be an open book, I just needed to find the right angle.

"Chloe, you're the town doctor. You're running your own business. On your own."

"So are you."

"Yes, well, that's neither here nor there."

"Oh, come on. The market went well, you said so yourself."

Because she didn't need to worry about me, I may have stretched the truth about how well I truly did. Numbers didn't lie the way I did, and red wasn't a great colour, on me or the books.

"You're going to do big things. And you don't need anyone's help." There was a hint of jealousy in her voice, which was rare.

Suddenly, it dawned on me, especially about the help. "You talked to her today, didn't you?"

She twisted her head so fast to stare me down that I worried she'd need a chiropractor for an adjustment. "No."

"Liar."

Our server dropped off the wine and casually mentioned he'd return.

Chloe crossed her legs and took a sip of the wine. "Fine. But it wasn't very long."

"Just long enough for Carleen to chirp. What did she say this time?"

Dr. Carleen Dewitt, her wicked stepmother, was the number one reason Chloe left the family business and moved five hours away. Carleen always thought the worst of Chloe, and never held back in vocalizing her concerns. Chloe and I both knew it was a form of emotional and verbal abuse, but Chloe never had the strength to fight against it and would only grip my hand to stop me from running off the mouth when I was present for the attacks. Carleen was a horrible person, and there was no nice way to say it.

As it always happened when the conversation rolled back to the stepmother, Chloe lost her remaining zest. "She claims I'm going to fail miserably, and she expects me home in a month. Small-town doctors go broke quickly as there isn't the patient load to carry them."

I laughed out loud, and a couple of diners turned in my direction. Quieting myself down, I inhaled. "She can't be serious? She knows how this all works. You signed a year-long contract with the Doctors of BC."

"I know that, but she's right, I'm not getting new patients."

"So what? You have a full supply of current patients."

"But some are switching to the doctor over here in Spirit Bay."

"Their loss." Honestly, it was.

Chloe's medical approach wasn't a hand-holding one, she was direct, but also kind and nurturing, always going above and beyond for her patients.

She waved my comment away. "I don't want to talk about work. Or Carleen. I need a solid distraction from my life, that's why I hired Justin."

"Even if you can't have him?" I whispered. "Sexually."

She sighed a soul-crushing sigh. "He's so yummy, and the arm porn he gave. Wow."

"Whoa, whoa, whoa." I leaned closer and narrowed my gaze. "What the hell is arm porn?"

A dreaminess softened her features and wiped away the wrinkled tension around her eyes. "When a guy wears a dress shirt, but he uncuffs it and rolls it up his forearms. It just magically displays this awesomeness, especially when his arms are toned and defined." She breathed out and the sparkle in her eyes returned. "I'd love to explore more and give him a truly intimate physical."

"Chloe." My eyes bugged out ten times their size with her confession.

"I'm getting tired of solo practice." She winked, but there was a ribbon of a whine in her words. "I need a partnership. What if I decided to not keep Justin on staff? Could I have him then? Or at least a dozen nights of seductive and sensual connections?"

I reached for my best friend's hand and looked her deep in the eyes. "Chloe, was there anything in the interview that would lead you to believe he was even interested?"

She broke her gaze and ran her finger along the rim of her wine glass. "I don't know, maybe?"

"Don't act on it unless you're 100% sure." I took a sip and

muttered. "And maybe not even then. Relationships with coworkers is a bottle of yuck." A road I'd been all too familiar with. "Promise me you won't."

"I can't." She took a sip of her wine.

"You asked him out already, didn't you?"

"We're going dancing. Nothing big, right? You and Adam were dancing the other night."

"Well, that's different."

"How? Didn't it lead somewhere?" She raised her brow.

"Chloe, I brought you home, remember? We traded places, and I became your wingman." She'd had a lot to drink that night, but I didn't think she'd forgotten it all.

"Right." She bobbed her head slowly. "Anyway, nice deflect by the way, what's up with you and Adam?"

"Nothing." I avoided her gaze and flipped open the menu.

"But there's something?" She reached across the table and pulled the menu out from under me.

I shook my head. "Why? What do you think is going on?"

A small snort escaped her. "You're a fool if you don't see it."

"Then I'm a fool." I ran my finger along the top of the wine glass, daring it to sing.

"Summer…" She lifted my hand away from the glass and gave it a tender squeeze. "It's okay, you know, to like someone else."

"Is it?" My ocean view blurred. "Because it feels wrong. Not wrong in the sense that you would think it's wrong, but wrong in the sense that I don't know if I'm ready."

94

After Declan, and how he'd broken my trust so many times, I wasn't sure I was ready to dole it out. Or if I even had any left.

"Adam's a good guy."

"I know he is." He's shown me multiple times in so many different ways.

"And he seems to really like you." A soft, sympathetic smile stretched across her face.

I wanted to casually throw the *why me?* question out into the universe, but I didn't actually want to hear any answers. "He'd be better off with someone else."

"Doesn't he get to be the one to make that call?"

"It's too soon, Chloe. I can't. I can't let someone into my heart. I don't know if I could take it being broken like that again."

"Declan tried."

My blurry tears of sadness became red hot with anger. She only saw the show and didn't know what went on behind the scenes. It wasn't her fault. I hadn't told her the truth, and she'd hate me forever if she knew.

My eyes went large. "Wait. A. Minute. You don't think I was purposely...? I mean, you don't really think...?"

"You and Declan had a chemistry that was really something to watch, from an outsider's point of view."

We had put on an Oscar-worthy performance and had everyone believing in the lie, but in the end, it cost me. Everything. Chloe had no idea just how broken I truly was; emotionally, mentally, and financially.

"All I ever told him was how I enjoyed being his friend. That's all." My voice found some strength from the surging flashes of resentment. Rehashing the biggest mistake in my life was not something I enjoyed having thrown back into my face.

"It's okay." She scanned the restaurant, warning me we had spectators. "Take a deep breath."

I inhaled loudly through my nose, and as I slowly exhaled, I felt a calmness blanket me. After all, I'd been practicing that move for longer than I knew. "We're not here to talk about that, but we are here to celebrate a birthday. Right?"

"Right."

Birthdays had been Andre's favourite, and it didn't matter who; co-workers, his boss, his teacher, or our friends. If he knew it was your birthday, he went out of his way to make it special. He was one of kind who, unfortunately, didn't get to celebrate many of his own.

The tears I'd held back burst free. They always did as far as Andre was concerned. "He would've been twenty-eight."

Andre, my first and only love, my fiancé, who had fought cancer, but lost.

"I know." She moved chairs and sat beside me, wiping away my river. Gently patting my hand, she nodded to the ocean. "He would've loved this place, wouldn't he have?"

I stared out to the ocean. It had been his dream, and mine too, to one day have an ocean-front property where we could watch the sunset every night. He loved the water and often claimed he was a merman in another life. Yeah, he would've been a repeat customer here, likely at this table with this view. He would've loved this restaurant and the whole bay area.

Chloe raised her wine glass. "To Andre."

"To Andre." We clinked them together.

"Do you want to know what I'm thinking?"

I gave my head a little shake and avoided looking into her sympathetic eyes. "Not really."

"I think it's time to move on, I really do. You're starting over and starting fresh. It's a great time to get back on the horse, and I see no better guy to try moving forward with than Adam."

Turning away from the ocean and giving her my undivided attention, I sighed as I covered my heart. "What if it doesn't work out?"

She tipped her forehead to mine. "If you keep putting up your walls, you'll never find out."

But making that leap was the hardest thing imaginable. There was no safety net and falling was life-altering. I'd already died once and wasn't sure I wanted to risk it again.

# Chapter Twelve

R eliving that horrible part of my past haunted my dreams for the next few days, and I felt as if I were walking around in a complete fog. Leaving the city of Victoria behind to start fresh was supposed to be a great thing, and yet, I was constantly hounded by feelings of failure and inadequacy. That I wasn't good enough in either my business or my personal life. That I'd never heal and be whole again.

Chloe was right about one thing - Adam was definitely the cream of the crop. A real genuine kind of guy, the kind where I couldn't get him out of my head despite all the effort I'd put into it, and believe me, I'd put a *lot* of effort into trying.

Saturday morning, at the break of the most gorgeous dawn I'd ever witnessed in Cheshire Bay, diving into my work became my sole focus. As I reminded myself of what I'd said to Chloe about how a man wasn't going to make her whole because she was already, I took the message to my own heart. Since there was no point in even trying to put myself out there, I remained steadfast in my determination to keep my heart safe and tightly protected. It was never going to be whole. And no one would be able to fill the void Andre left. The only thing that would help was work. Solid hard work would get my blood pumping. And that started with setting up my baby – the Bayside Market.

Kyle, the rental guy, motored down the road, and I fingered the card in my back pocket, wondering if I was going to be able to snag a deal.

As he pulled into the parking lot, my heart beat faster. The ideas swirling in my head were akin to a tornado – and most of them didn't make sense in the dark gusts of thoughts.

He hopped out and sauntered over to the back of the cargo van where he unhooked and rolled up the door. "Three carts of tables, two of chairs, correct?"

I nodded, my blood pumping at a breakneck speed as I scanned the darkened area for the tents until I settled on multiple stacks in the back "What would your price be for the tents? For today?"

"How many?" His gaze washed over me.

"Twenty-seven."

He climbed into the van and counted, mumbling the whole time.

I had some cash, but when he started scratching his head, I worried it wouldn't be enough. Finally, he tossed out an amount that exceeded my budget.

"Are they booked for today?"

"No."

Perfect. They weren't being used anyway, so a deal was a possibility, if I came at it from the right angle. The one I'd been trained to use. "Is there anything else I can offer instead? I have about half of what you're asking. In cash."

His gaze ran up and down my body. "I'm sure we can work out something."

I met his gaze, not willing to back down. Unfortunately, this was a road I'd been down before, but years of experience had made me a good negotiator. "What did you have in mind?"

He licked his lips. "I'm sure you can think of something, honey."

"Not for that." I cocked my brow and placed a hand on my hip. I knew what he was thinking, neon signs didn't give as much away. "For that kind of deal, I'd need the tents every week from now until the end of September. For free."

"You ain't that good, lady."

"And you'll never know."

He narrowed his gaze and stepped closer. "Is that a fact?"

I refused to answer – let him think what he wanted – but I also refused to open the distance between us and give him the power. "The tents?"

The air crackled, and he stared until I tipped my head toward the pile.

Finally, he shifted on his feet. "You can have them for the

rest of the month at half price, in cash, but I want a date. With you."

The joke was on him. "I don't date, and besides, there are two Saturdays left, including today, so no deal."

"Until May long weekend then." Desperation oozed in his tone, which was surprising. His attitude wasn't the best, but he wasn't unattractive. Likely with a shave and a shower, he'd clean up decently.

"What you're saying is, I would get the tents for half price for the next five Saturdays, as long as I agree to go out on a date with you?" The word *date* soured in my stomach.

Flashing lights went off in my head, and I constantly reminded myself *this* was a business transaction, and absolutely nothing more. There was no romance or anything. This deal had as much luck moving forward into a relationship as I had of spontaneously turning into a goat. Fighting to catch my breath so he wouldn't know the power had shifted in his favour, I tapped my foot to slow it down.

It would only be a few hours at most, and it would save my business a lot of money. The tents would give the market a polished look, hopefully attracting more vendors to sign up, and increasing the business. As the business grew, I could even implement a minimal fee to enter. Most customers wouldn't balk at a couple of dollars, and it would be a great way to build some petty cash, and by that point, I may not even need to make such stupid deals.

"One date?"

The bile rose in the back of my throat. Inhaling slowly and

methodically, I gave Kyle a subtle nod. This was business, not pleasure. "Assuming you agree to a few conditions, I think we can make the arrangement work."

"What conditions?" He tipped his head to the side like a dog did.

I searched the area to ensure we were still alone, and raised my hand, tapping my right finger against my left one as I counted out the rules. "First off, there will be no kissing or sex. Second, you pay your way, and I'll pay mine. That, and I'll be taking my own vehicle. I'll give you four hours for the evening which can include dinner and whatever else we mutually agree on, but it must be in a public venue. I promise to behave and give the illusion of having fun."

"Geez, lady, don't you trust me?"

"Nope." I pulled my shoulders back. "And this arrangement will take place at the end of the five weeks."

He scoffed and pulled his head back in disbelief. "Absolutely not. How do I know you'll uphold your word?"

"You'll have to trust me."

"Right. We've already established you don't trust me."

"Precisely, however, I will be paying you cash every week for the tents, so you won't have to declare that rental on your taxes. You're already making money; this bonus deal happens to be a kickback."

"Then it needs to happen within a couple of weeks, as an act of good faith."

"And you'll keep your word on the tent deal?"

"You can report me to CRA if I don't." Kyle had an indignant look on his face. I highly doubted he paid taxes, but it was good to know he knew the right terms. Maybe there was more to him than I thought.

"Fine."

I opened my phone's calendar with a muted sigh. Shit. I had plans to go with Adam to the regatta next Saturday. Oh god, what would he do if he knew I'd agreed to a *date* with this guy after I'd been turning him down for weeks? He could never find out. Didn't he say he worked late doing inventory one night a week? What day was that again? Tuesdays?

"I have an opening on May 3. It's a Tuesday night." Chloe was also out of town for a convention, so it worked doubly in my favour. Adam was doing inventory, Chloe was gone, and no one would ever find out.

"A weeknight?"

"My schedule doesn't allow me any room on a weekend until May long. The market is very time and labour consuming."

He sighed. "Fine. I'll give you the details next Saturday. But you won't cancel?"

"My word is my bond."

"You got the cash?"

I withdrew a pile of folded bills and handed it over. He shook my hand and started unloading the rentals while my insides turned into a slimy, sticky mush. I'd just prostituted myself for my business. I thought I'd left that practice behind in Victoria.

# Chapter Thirteen

O nce Kyle's cube van had left the parking lot, I ran over to the garbage and threw up, beyond disgusted at what I'd done, and what door to the past I had largely thrown open. However, there wasn't too much time to dwell on it as I had twenty-seven tents to assemble, plus tables and chairs to ready before the vendors arrived, and time was ticking.

Fighting to pop up the first tent, I was a little overwhelmed by how time-consuming it was. Really, it was a two-person job, but I was all alone and had to push through.

By the time I'd got the fifth tent up, I was starting to get the hang of it, however, I still had another twenty-two to go, plus all the tables and chairs, and it had already cost me an hour. No way was I getting it all done on time.

Finding a rush of energy from deep inside, I mentally planned on getting all the tents assembled first, and then doubling back to set up the tables. If nothing else, the vendors could assist with that, but I was hoping to not have to ask them for help. What kind of special event specialist would I be to ask such a thing? A lousy one.

As I was fighting with tent number twenty, trying to get the corner to lock into place as my arms had expended all their strength, the first vendor rumbled over the parking lot.

"Damn it."

Just my luck, Adam jumped out and came over.

"I've got it, thanks." And with a grunt, I popped it into place.

"Have you assembled all of these yourself?" He whistled as he glanced around.

Tired, I snapped out a sarcastic reply but made sure my tone was lighter than I was feeling. "Do you see anyone else?"

He laughed. "Let me help."

Defeated, my shoulders rolled forward.

"Or I can let you do it all on your own, if you prefer." He stood with his arms crossed over his strong chest, a sardonic smile itching to stretch across his unshaven face.

I walked over to the next tent and unzipped the bag, making sure the legs were properly positioned. I pulled one side open and walked over to the other side to open it further. Extending the legs, one by one, I kept a side eye on Adam, who just stood there. Until I couldn't find the strength to push the tent up. Apparently popping open and setting up twenty tents was my upper limit.

Ready to burst into tears from frustration, Adam finally walked over and with ease, locked it into position.

"Easy for you." The retort was quick and snappy.

"You did all the hard work." His smile was soft and settled my frayed nerves.

I checked the time on my watch. Vendors were allowed to start arriving in a few minutes, and I felt no closer to being ready for them. No tables and chairs were set up. Not even all the tents. But there wasn't time to wallow in self-pity. On to the next tent.

Adam stood beside me as I pulled the tent free of the bag and with us on either side, we wordlessly sprung it open and had it set up in a fraction of time, with Adam locking everything into place.

"Thanks," I muttered. "That was much easier."

"You didn't even need to ask for help." He winked.

Together, and magically, we had the rest of the tents set up before the vendors arrived.

All that remained were the tables and chairs.

As we were setting up the first ones, Libby and Erin arrived. "Can we grab our tables?"

I stood up straight and avoided looking at Erin, especially as Adam came and stood beside me. "Of course. Sorry it's not already done."

Next week would be different. Jokingly a wild thought crossed my warped mind – maybe if I flashed Kyle, he'd help me set up. He made it sound like it wasn't too big a deal previously.

"Oh, no worries. We don't mind." Libby bounced around, and I wondered if I used her energy to finish setting up, how long it would take? Minutes likely. "You've already done the tents. Were those an additional fee?"

I knew and understood that tone. "Not likely, as I have other ways of covering the cost. For now."

"It's a huge expense," Erin said, as she pulled a table off the cart.

I shrugged and looked down the line. Maybe, but it was worth it. The market looked so much better with the tents – gave it a polished, curbside appeal, plus it provided shade for the hard workers. Next season, assuming I was in the black at the end of this one, it was reasonable to increase the vendor's weekly fee. I had the summer to figure out what worked and what didn't, and to plan accordingly. An entrance fee would also seriously help offset the additional costs.

"Where are we this week?" Libby asked.

Oh shit. Because they had arrived before I was ready, I hadn't put their names in the spots.

"Go," Adam said, waving me off.

My clipboard was back at my pile of stuff at the entrance to the market. Huffing and puffing, I grabbed a roll of tape and hurried back to Adam, Erin, and Libby. Erin was talking as I approached but quickly sealed her lips when I got within earshot. It wasn't hard to assume she'd been talking about me. Although I felt I hadn't done anything wrong, I wanted to get on her good side.

"Tell you what." I looked at the layout. "Since you were here first, and you're taking a table to set up, you pick where you want to go."

Erin flipped her gaze between Libby and Adam. "What if we

set up near the front, where all the traffic is, where they'll want your food, and then they may stop again on the way out... But if we set up in the middle..."

I tried to hold back my impatience as she jumped back and forth, debating the merits of the most ideal spot, which was why I normally had this done. My trying to be nice was backfiring while I lost valuable set-up time in her painstaking decision making.

Finally, she picked a spot, four tables in, with Sylvia's Bakery beside her.

I swapped their places on my map with the other vendors and stole a look at Adam.

"I'll finish setting and dropping off tables and chairs."

"Where do you want to set up?" After all, I'd offered it to his sister.

That infectious, light up your insides smile returned, and I knew why I'd fallen under his spell at the bar, each and every time. It was captivating and carefree and had a power over me. If I wasn't strong enough, I just may give in to his charm, something I kept vowing wouldn't happen.

He tapped the clipboard. "Where do you have me?"

"You make it so difficult sometimes." I playfully punched his shoulder.

"Thank you, I really try." He winked.

Fighting to hold myself together, I showed him my layout and pointed out his spot.

"I'm happy there. It's perfect."

Which was true. Of all the vendors, his was the one I'd spent the most time planning and making sure it was the ideal location.

"Go hang your signs."

"But the tables…" We hadn't even gotten started and vendors were arriving.

"Get that handled," he pointed to my clipboard, "and then come back. I'm not going anywhere." An easy smile bloomed, pushing up the corners of his eyes.

"Really?" It was such an odd assortment of words to throw out, however with my physical energy zapped, my mental energy was taking a hit, one comment at a time. If I didn't get him out of my personal space soon, we were both in big trouble.

Flying around the market, I propped up everyone's name on their tent, greeted the incoming vendors, and somehow managed to make it over to Adam before he'd finished setting up his own space.

"That was pretty remarkable."

I couldn't stop myself. "Watching me, were you?"

The faint blush stole his composure, and he tipped his head down to extend the legs on the folding table. I didn't miss the side-eyed stares and sly, little smile.

With everything set up, I sent him on his way, watching him disappear into the excited crowds as people milled about. I was supposed to be avoiding him and instead I couldn't stop myself from keeping a close eye on his sexy body and his even sweeter demeanour.

Maybe Chloe had been right. Damn her and her seed planting.

As he was wheeling his dolly to his table, he stopped at mine. "By the way, this is for you."

I took the coffee from his hand. "Thank you. You're very sweet always bringing me something."

"Ah, don't get too excited. It's cold now, but–"

I patted his arm, letting my fingers linger a touch too long. "Trust me, it'll hit the spot. Thank you for your help. I truly appreciate it."

"I know you do, even if you won't ask for it."

"That's not true."

"Can I help you tear everything down?" There was a glint in his eyes I'd never noticed before.

"Nah, that's easy."

"See what I mean?"

I pressed my lips together in a mock pout. "But I can do it. I'm more than capable."

"I'm not doubting that. All I'm saying is we make a good team."

Something I couldn't deny, even if I wanted to. However, teamwork got me into trouble once before, and I was damned if I was going to let it happen ever again.

Refusing to leave me alone to do the grunt work, Adam helped me take down all the tents. Most of the vendors had been kind enough to load their tables and chairs onto the carts, so packing up the tents seemed pretty stress-free. Plus, it wasn't as strength-draining since they collapsed easier than assembling.

"Thanks again for your help, Adam."

"Thanks for not kicking me to the curb."

"And why would I do that?" I placed my calloused hands on my hips.

Adam cleared his throat. "You seem to be the kind of person who refuses help and it's got me thinking about why."

I swallowed, but since I didn't want him to see my expression changing, I twisted and closed my bins, stacking them behind my car.

"Either you want all the fame and glory to yourself." My eyes widened at such a wild accusation. "Which doesn't seem to fit your personality, or, and this is the most likely, you're a head-strong woman who is just obstinately stubborn." He drawled out the last two words with a grin and helped me load the last of my boxes into my trunk. "So, which is it?"

My gaze danced between his soulful eyes, where Father Time had stamped a little age onto the edges. "Neither. I just do it myself because it's easier to do it than having to explain to anyone else what my thought process is on set up, or worse, having to explain why I want it that way."

"Uh-huh, I see."

I raised my right shoulder and circled it through the air. What I really needed was a hot shower to loosen the knot.

"You okay?"

"Shoulder aches. I got all my cardio today, plus all my arm

workouts are done." I winked and closed the trunk. Thank goodness tomorrow was my one day off. I was pretty sure I wasn't going to be able to lift my arms higher than waist height.

"Let me?" He signalled for me to turn around, which I, surprisingly, found myself doing.

His strong hands settled on my right shoulder, and he gently dug his thumbs into my shoulder blade.

A low groan washed out as I braced myself against my car for support. "That feels great."

But it was more than just his thumbs smoothing out the knot; it was the heated feeling flowing under his hands as they covered my shoulders. Warmth radiated down the length of my arms, adding electrified pulses to the tips of my fingers.

Time lost all meaning the longer he kneaded into my aching muscles, and I involuntarily moaned.

He leaned close. His whiskers tickled my cheeks and the heat from his breath warmed my already searing ears. "That sound will be my undoing."

I tensed and went as straight as a pole. "What? Oh my god, sorry. I didn't mean to–"

I hadn't meant to make my moans sound seductive, it was just a natural side effect, and Jesus Christ, I'd thought I'd kept them under wraps. Apparently not. God damn it! Flustered, I paced away from him and surveyed the area, making sure there wasn't a piece of garbage anywhere.

"Yep, all good," I said to no one.

Assured the space was in the same condition as I got it, I strode back to my car and opened the passenger door, pausing for a heartbeat to take in a confused Adam. "Look, I'm sorry about the sounds. I didn't mean to lead you on."

"Would that be such a bad thing?" The crease between his brows deepened as his arms boxed me in.

"Yes."

"Because it's me?"

I ached a little at seeing his face crinkle. I wanted to reach out and touch his arm in comfort, but not at the expense of sending the wrong message. "Trust me, it's all me."

He sighed and shook his head, looking skyward. "The whole *it's not you, it's me* cliché."

"It's true. I just can't... won't... It doesn't work." Words failed me, and the weight of not being able to string together a proper sentence pushed on my shoulders. The dull ache returned.

Adam rocked back and forth on his heels and thrust his hands into the pockets of his jeans. "What am I going to do with you?" It was said with the highest tone and the sweetest inflection.

"Nothing. I'm not worth it." It wasn't said so he'll fawn all over me and say all the right things he probably thought I'd wanted to hear while also having some pity on the predicament I somehow always seemed to find myself in. It was the cold hard truth.

"I beg to differ." His eyes darted to the rental van driving down the gravel road to where we were standing. "Your rental guy is here."

Finally, Kyle arrived to collect his things. After backing towards us, he rolled up the door.

Adam pushed a cart closer to the van as Kyle presented me with a clipboard, the pad of his fingertip grazing my hand.

"What's this?" I stared at Kyle, fighting the churn of my stomach.

"A write-up of our earlier agreement." His gaze jumped from the clipboard to Adam and back to me.

Turning to check, I watched as Adam walked to the furthest cart and pushed it toward the loading ramp. I didn't have much time.

Taking a quick look, I started scanning the document, but I didn't get too far.

"Everything okay?"

I dropped the clipboard. Somehow, Adam had appeared by my side. Seriously, how fast did the guy move?

Picking up the agreement, I kept it face down. "Oh, yeah. Just working out the details for the tents for the next few weeks. I've secured a deal until the long weekend."

"Oh, that's fantastic. Hope he gave you a good deal."

I didn't know how to answer and didn't dare chance a look at either guy.

"I need you to sign it." Kyle offered me a pen from his pocket.

A shudder coursed through me as I touched his fingers. I gave it a cursory glance, signed my name to the bottom, and grabbed my phone to take a picture, angling it so Adam couldn't read any of it.

"Trying to not get a reflection." My cheeks burned as I

positioned the clipboard and snapped a copy for my personal records.

Kyle took the clipboard back and tossed it into the van.

"We're good?" I didn't need to watch him load the carts. I had my own issues to work on.

"Yeppers. See you next week."

I nodded and led Adam back over to my car.

"Rental guys, eh?" I rolled my eyes.

"About earlier, when I asked what I'm going to do with you…"

I shrugged and avoided locking onto his gaze. Instead, I threw it over to the field we'd just packed up, making sure it was in as good condition as when I'd arrived that morning. "I can't, Adam. I'm just not a relationship girl. I don't have time." My cheeks were getting a substantial workout. "Work comes first."

"Wow." He took a step back and tipped his head to the side. "Really?"

I pressed my lips together and inhaled to calm the pounding of my heart. A piteous expression shadowed Adam's face, and it was slowly breaking my heart. "Thank you again for your assistance. See you next week?"

"I said I'd be here, right?" And without another word, he turned and stalked over to his truck.

Well, I deserved that, didn't I? At least I was honest and left no wandering doubt about my intentions. What was the matter with me? I actually liked Adam.

# Chapter Fourteen

Biting against the deep aches in my arms which were still giving me a hard time two days later, I pushed open the door to A Whole New World, while balancing two coffees from Java & Lattes: truly the best coffee in all of Cheshire Bay. The bells above the door sounded, and once again I was transported to a someplace new. The scent of books lingered in the air, mixed with a spicy cinnamon smell, and a low murmur of whispering voices came from the side.

I spotted Adam at the counter, leaning over the computer, his fingers punching the keys, obviously deep in thought.

I cleared my throat as I approached. "Good morning. For you."

"What for?"

"A peace offering?" Not sure why I rose my voice at the end. Since he didn't take the coffee, I set it beside the keyboard.

He looked at the drink and then up at me. "Thanks."

"So, I was thinking." I searched his face, hoping that familiar light in his eyes would return, instead I met darkness. I'd really screwed up, but I had a plan. "You mentioned that you couldn't do author signings because the space is so tight in here."

There was barely room to move between the rows of shelves, so a gathering of two dozen people to meet an author was absolutely out of the question.

Adam continued clicking on the computer, but at least he'd taken a sip of his drink – a maple latte, one of my personal favourites.

"Which got me thinking," I carried on.

Two young ladies approached the counter with a stack of books, so I stepped off to the side. Paying customers came first.

An insincere smile tipped the corner of Adam's lips up as he rang up their purchase and bagged the books, adding in bookmarks and a receipt. The girls giggled in hushed whispers as the one brazenly touched Adam's hand, and her friend's eye went large. Neither was courageous enough to have said more than a weak *thanks* before they left the store.

"Cute," I said. "They were quite smitten with you."

"Yeah, right. They're always like that."

"Because they like you."

"And they're about fifteen years too young." Which was true. They were definite high schoolers, if that. His voice was terse, like hot blades on thin ice. "You said you'd been thinking about something?"

"Right." I walked back in front of the counter and pulled out

117

my random idea pad. "Well, I was looking at my booked author signings and wanted to do a joint venture with you. They'll be at the market on Saturday, but what if we – or A Whole New World – also hosted them for an exclusive reading and book signing."

"Aren't the readers getting that at the market?"

"Not the reading, and hopefully the foot traffic keeps him or her busy where there's not a lot of chatting going on."

"A book signing, as wonderful as that would be, it just doesn't make financial sense to do it outside the market, which is six hours long, and hundreds of people moving through. I have a store capacity of fifty-six but the way everything is set up, if twenty can fit, it'd be tight. Your market idea was brilliant and is a much better deal for the author." He refocused on his computer screen.

"My plan was to make the book signing exclusive."

"You've lost me." He took a sip of his coffee and finally tore his gaze away from the monitor.

Slightly taken back that he wasn't as excited as I was about the idea, I scoffed slightly. "The plan was we make it exclusive on the Friday night. A real intimate gathering. You could make it a lottery. Make a purchase during the week, get an entry. Purchase any of the author's backlist books, so as to not take away from their new release, and they get five entries. Or sell tickets for a buck each. Or something similar as there are a million ways to go about the lottery-type of draw. Then on the Friday afternoon, you post the winners on your social media, which would help in building your business, and they get to come and meet the author early, and hang out without a busy market crowd. The author gets to enjoy the fans. It's a win-win for all involved."

"Where? Here?" He waved a hand around as a deep frown formed an even deeper V on his forehead.

"No, because I understand the space limitation." I inhaled and held my breath to calm my words. I was so excited, and somehow, he seemed to not be reading into it as I would've liked. "I've asked various places around town, and three were willing to close their space for a couple of hours for a very modest fee, to give exclusivity, on the condition that the customers buy something while inside. Here's a small list of available places." Steadying my nerves, I slid the piece of paper in his direction.

He picked it up and gazed upon it. "Really? They'll close for a couple of hours?"

"Yep."

"On a Friday night?" He tapped his chin with his long finger as a pensive expression settled over him. "These aren't huge name authors though."

The list of local authors included many best-selling and widely-known writers, however, none of them returned my inquiry. The lesser-known, more indie-based authors were another story, and were totally excited to jump on board with my plan.

"You're correct, but these ones," I tapped the paper near the bottom, "they'd love to meet with fans and readers and build their base. If they're going to be in the area anyhow, why not sweeten the pot for them? I can have the authors bring just their latest release for the market days, and you provide the backlist for the Friday night ticket event."

"You can do something like that?"

"Of course. I'd need to contact them to see who'd be spending the night and propose the idea and make amendments to the contract. I highly doubt all will agree, but I think it's a safe assessment to say most would."

He shook his head and turned his attention back to the computer. "I guess we'll see."

The air was thick and hung between us, and I got the sneaking suspicion from his lack of interest, that he wasn't on board. Although I wasn't upset, per se, it still stung a little. "If you don't think it'll work, I take no offense. It was just something I came up with."

"Tell you what, I'll think on it and talk it over with Grandpa." He glanced toward the ceiling.

"Excellent. Keep me posted."

He looked deep into my eyes, such an intoxicating pull. "What's in this for you? It's a lot of work for you to not get much out of it."

"While that may be true since I am trying to find my place in the area, I'm putting on all the hats. Market co-ordinator, special event manager, anything and everything, for now, to drive a steady income. I even had someone approach me to help plan a wedding, but I draw the line there. Brides can be the worst." However, there would be good money to be made, because as long as you attached the word wedding to something you could charge an arm and a leg, and most wouldn't balk about it.

"Yes, they can."

Although it was muttered under his breath, there was a nasty undercurrent in the deep throb of his voice. Had his ex-wife been a bridezilla?

Shaking away the thought of him looking like a million dollars in a black tuxedo with his hair perfectly styled and his face clean-shaven so the eyes popped, I tug through my portfolio. I pulled out another sheet with the authors and the weeks they were scheduled to appear at the market and handed it to him.

"You gave me this already."

"Oh?" I tipped my head quickly. "My apologies." I went to take it back and my fingers grazed his.

I followed the length of his hand and settled on his bare arm with his dress shirt sleeve rolled up to the elbow – *arm porn* as Chloe had mentioned – and suddenly, I saw the appeal. And the attraction. Well defined, the sight of his naked arm stirred something deep, but it was his smile and the crinkle of his eyes as he took me that did all the work. That heat warmed me up from the inside out.

"I should get going." The words choked out, and an embarrassed pitch in my voice highlighted that. Seriously, what was going on with me?

I stepped back, putting a much-needed gap between us, and smoothed my hands over my hair as I suddenly felt like I was falling apart.

Before I could step away any further, he cleared his throat

and searched my face. "Are we still on for Saturday's regatta?"

There were a million excuses at my disposal. It was a Saturday after all, and I'd likely be tired and sore from tent assembly and just the general running around from the market as it pushed me harder each week. Plus, there was always work to be done on the social media front – couldn't make Bayside Market a successful endeavor if I wasn't on it all the time. But the biggest reason for my hesitation was surprisingly simple and truly asinine – I had nothing appropriate to wear.

So many reasons to say no.

But when I looked at the sweet expression tugging on his lips and the corners of his eyes turned skyward with hope, I caved. "You bet."

I hadn't expected my answer to have such a spring in its step.

# Chapter Fifteen

Chloe leaned her arm against the frame of the bathroom. "You should wear your hair up, like in a ponytail or something. It would work better with that dress."

What my hair needed was to be cut into a 1950's style to match, but that was never going to happen. I left it down in its naturally wavy state, the length of it hung below my shoulder blades, giving the vintage dress a more modern spin.

From the moment Chloe purchased the dress, I had wanted to wear it but never found the occasion. After months of it being neglected in her closet, I was finally going to get the chance to use it. The top was a little loose, even with my push-up bra, and the little cap sleeves were just perfect – a huge change from the normal jeans and tee style I traditionally wore. With it on, I felt regal and ladylike.

"What about a necklace?" Chloe pulled out a gold chain from her jewelry box.

"I'll go bare. I don't want to be too noticeable, after all, this feels like an undercover mission or something." As it was, my makeup was minimal, and my fingernails weren't painted.

"So having fun is totally out of the question?" Chloe cocked an eyebrow and tugged at the collar of her sweatshirt.

"To a degree."

My plan was simple – check out the event, make tons of mental notes, and blend in, all while making sure I kept an emotional distance from my – what could I call him? *My date* seemed completely out of context, and *my companion* didn't have the right ring. *Just some guy?* Yeah, that was weird too.

Refocusing on my reflection, I nodded, pleased with my appearance. I spun around.

"You look gorgeous. Adam should adore you."

"I don't want him to adore me. This isn't a date." Something he had confirmed yesterday, as we talked more about the book signings.

"Oh-kay."

It grated on my nerves when she split that word into two distinct syllables. "What's that supposed to mean?"

"It's a date, Summer, like it or not. You're going out for dinner and dancing and a good time. With a handsome guy, I might add."

"It's a work thing, I've told you that. Besides, after everything that happened…"

She squeezed my forearm in a reassuring, big-sister-like way. "I know." She brushed the hair off my shoulders and stood behind me, tipping her head against mine. "He's different, and I know you see that too. Patient and sweet and somehow totally on board with your absolutely insane refusal for anything to become more."

"Yeah, well…"

"Would it be the worst thing in the world if you classified tonight as a date-date?"

I stared at her through the reflection in the mirror, trying to stop my face from contorting into any expression that could be misrepresented. "I don't know."

"I know you, and I know you kissing him at the end of the evening would be a big step. Huge. But this, right now? This is just going out for dinner and dancing. Pretty harmless in the grand scheme of things, right? People do that all the time. We do it. Besides, it's just a word – a date. You've set dates on your calendar for events and appointments, how is this any different?" A sympathetic yet sad smile started across her lips.

"Because when you say two people are on a date it has expectations. It means something, like flowers and schmaltz. And kissing."

But she was right to a small degree. It was just an umbrella title to put over top of an activity. I swallowed and listened to the pounding of my heart. Calling it something different wouldn't change what was about to go on tonight, I just had to be upfront about the whole romance part of it.

"Okay." My head bobbled like a toy. "Let's call it a date."

I waited for my heart to explode, and when nothing happened,

I released my breath.

Chloe kissed my shoulder. "He's a lucky guy."

"No. I'm the lucky one." I squeezed her hand.

"You can do this."

I stepped into the hallway and walked with purpose into my room, trying to wrap myself in bravado. "How's Justin doing?"

"Ugh." She fell onto my mattress and let her head hit the pillow, blonde hairs flying in all directions. "He may be good looking, and an animal in the sack—"

"So that's who was over last night." My eyes widened. There was a fair amount of noise coming from her room, but I honestly didn't think it was one of her staff.

"I couldn't help it. He's solid."

"He's also your employee. Do you know how many ethical rules you're breaking? Maybe they'll go over them at the convention on Monday."

"Oh relax, Norma Rae. I gave Justin his walking papers on Thursday." She curled herself into a sitting position. "He's buff, but he's not too bright. This morning I expanded the reach of my ad. Maybe someone will be willing to move here for the job. I am paying competitively with lots of perks. Until then, Darla has agreed to come back."

Something I believed she'd do. "I wish I knew how to help you."

She semi-snorted and smoothed out the comforter. "I need someone like you. A self-starter, a go-getter. Look at you, you've been here less than two months and you've already hit your minimum business goals."

If only she knew how deep in debt I truly was. I was going to be pinching pennies to pay for rent, as I was way past living beyond my means. Just yesterday I called the credit card company and asked for an increase on my limit.

Her tone turned to a self-deprecating one as she crossed her legs and folded her hands into her lap. "Maybe Carleen was right. Maybe I won't be able to do this on my own."

Damn her stepmother for having put those seeds in her head. The next time I saw her, I wasn't going to be so tight-lipped. The women deserved a serious reaming out.

"You are 100% able to do this on your own because you *are* doing it. Don't compare your solo, small-town practice to a metropolis, family-run one. They aren't even the same thing. And as for finding the right receptionist for the job, they're out there and will show themselves soon. I believe that with all my heart. And until then, Darla's agreed to stay on, so you're not alone."

The buzzer sounded and saved by the bell, Chloe leaped off the bed, wiggling her brows as she danced by me. "He's here."

My heart started pounding, kicking up a swarm of butterflies, and I double-checked my reflection in the mirror.

"Thought you weren't excited about your..." She hesitated. "Date?" She beamed and exited the room.

Adam knocked on the other side of the door, and I hesitated in answering. Inhaling sharply, I needed to calm myself first. One deep breath first. Then another.

Chloe nudged me. "Open it."

I smoothed out the flare of my shirt, suddenly worried I'd overdressed, while also hoping to tame the uptick in nervousness. Friends went on business dates all the time, and tonight was no different. Friends! That was the word I'd been looking for earlier. We were simply two friends with common interests out on a business arrangement.

Chloe opened the door and glared in my direction, while turning on the charm. "Hi, Adam. You look great."

Indeed, and great didn't even describe it. Dressed in dark grey pants with a matching suit jacket, and a simple white button-up with the top two buttons undone, he was classic. It was understated and yet stylish, and surprisingly, also took my breath away.

"Doesn't he look great, Summer?"

I nodded, but my lips failed to move.

"You'll have to forgive my friend," Chloe said as she ushered Adam inside the apartment. "She gets all dressed up and forgets how to talk."

"You look…" Adam stood stiffly; his mouth slightly open. "Wow. You look stunning."

I tipped my head down as heat flooded my cheeks. It had been years since anyone had paid me such a compliment. "Thank you, so do you."

I slipped into a pair of wedges to give my height a little boost.

"You two will be the hit of the festival, especially since you look perfect together." She giggled, and I wanted to die right there. "Don't forget your keys since I'm not waiting up, I have an early drive in the morning. Just sneak in like you did the last time you two hooked up."

Whipping my head around, I narrowed my eyes at Chloe.

I snatched my keys from the bowl and stuffed them into my purse before I pulled my jacket off the hanger.

"Please, allow me." Adam took the jacket and held it so I could slip my arms into it.

I pulled my trapped hair out to spill over the back, and quickly caught Chloe's look – she was taking in every second watching the two of us. "We should go."

"Nice to see you again, Dr. Tarkin." Adam held the door as we walked through.

Quickly I turned around as Chloe put her hands into a heart shape. My eyes went large, and I urgently waved her gesture away before Adam saw it.

"Have fun." Her high-pitched voice filled the hallway before the door clicked shut.

"You ready for tonight?" Adam said.

"I didn't have time to do much research, so I'll be taking notes." Why was I subtly reminding him how this was an undercover mission?

He laughed. "I didn't see a notebook or a laptop."

I tapped my temple as we descended the stairs. "Mental notes. Although I do have a little notepad in my purse."

"Well, you just may surprise yourself and have a little fun too."

On the second step down, I paused and inhaled sharply. "About tonight."

He stopped, and eye level to me searched my eyes. "Have you changed your mind?"

"Yes." I slowly nodded and watched as the joy he'd held a moment ago dropped onto the floor. "But not for what you're thinking." I couldn't bare to look at him, so I slithered my gaze down and settled on the collar of his shirt. Once again, I took a deep breath. "God this is hard."

"Just spit it out."

"Okay, okay." My goodness, why was I so nervous? I could do this. It was just a title change, and really, did it affect how the night would go? Maybe? Maybe not. "For tonight... Oh, good grief." My lungs filled with air, but I needed to push on despite the rush of blood racing through my body. "We can call tonight a date. If you want to."

Probably one of the hardest things I've had to vocalise in years, but it was out there. No turning back. The worst part was I looked at the floor like a child who'd been caught with a hand in the cookie jar. However, I chanced a small peek as I slowly rolled my gaze up.

A broad smirk pushed the left corner of his lips towards his smoldering gaze. "Why, Summer Bates, have you changed your mind about dating?"

I shook my head. "No." I inched my focus up to his eyes and rolled my bottom lip between my teeth. "But, for tonight, I'm... Well... I'm going to try."

He reached for my hand and lifted it to his lips, gently placing a kiss atop my quivering knuckles. "I promise to be a gentleman, and yet, show you a good time on your first official date. With me. You'll be safe and we'll have a blast, you'll see."

I got lost in the sincerity in the depths of his blues knowing what he said was the truth. We were going to have a good time, and somehow, deep down I knew I was safe.

We reached the main entrance and walked out into the fresh spring air. Sitting in visitor parking was a lone motorbike, and I glanced around to see if he'd maybe parked his truck in another stall.

"Hope you don't mind." Adam stopped at the bike and opened the back storage thing, passing me a helmet. "Had I known this was going to be a *date*–" He whispered the word and grimaced. "I would've brought a different mode of transportation. But I figured since we were going as friends, this would be more fun."

Already the word was pressing new meaning into things, and we hadn't even left the parking lot.

"I'll get my car. Just give me a minute." My heart was racing but not because of the handsome man before me holding out a helmet. "I'm really scared."

"About this being called something else or the mode of

transportation?"

"The motorcycle." I couldn't stop staring at it. "This is all new for me as I've never ridden on one in my life."

"Never?" Despite his disbelief in my comment, he carried on. "They're fun."

"And super scary."

"Not if the driver is responsible." He pulled his helmet on and adjusted the strap under his chin. "I've never had an accident, or even been close."

My eyes roamed the length of the motorbike. It wasn't a Tom Cruise-Top Gun style variety, more along the lines of what you'd see a dad drive, but it wasn't a Harley with its big handlebars. Truth be told, it did look rather stable, as far as bikes went, and it appeared heavier than my car, which was weird.

"Will an iron-clad promise to drive carefully ease your tension?"

A deep inhale expanded my chest.

"I'm really going to have to do more research on you. I don't know much about you, aside from your fear of water, your fear of heights, and now this." He tipped his head in genuine curiosity, all the while keeping a certain charm and sincerity in his voice. "What's this fear all about?"

"All of it. There's nothing separating me from the ground in the event of …" Finishing that sentence would surely jinx the situation, something we didn't need. There was already enough mounting pressure.

"How about a quick ride around the block? If it's too much, we'll come back and uber it over. Fair enough?"

Slowly, despite my hesitation, my head took the lead and nodded as my shaky hands reached for the helmet and dropped it on. Good thing I hadn't really done much with my hair as it was all going to be plastered to my head now.

Adam's fingers grazed my cheeks and jawline, sending pulses of electricity through my body, as he adjusted the chin strap and tapped his warm finger on the tip of my nose. "Cute."

I don't know what possessed me, but I curtsied at his comment.

Adam swung a leg over the bike and kicked up the kickstand, holding the bike firmly. "You're going to put your foot on that step and swing your leg over. Use me for balance and please trust me. I won't let anything happen."

As instructed, I did what he asked, white-knuckling his shoulder with a death grip while I lowered myself onto the seat and leaned into the backrest as he adjusted himself. I tucked my skirt under me.

"Ready?"

I wasn't. Not even close.

"You can hold onto me by wrapping your arms around my chest, or there are handles on either side of your seat."

The bike roared to life, and the engine revved as he twisted the throttle.

"Oh, one final note, lean the way I'm leaning whenever we

turn." He twisted his head to look at me. "Alright, you ready? One quick trip around the block. Less time than a rollercoaster ride."

It had been years since I'd been on a coaster, so I'd take him at his word. With a strength reserved for my Pilates class, my thighs gripped his hips as I held onto the handles. "Okay, let's do this."

Slowly, the bike moved, and we were on our way out of the parking lot. Never before had my heart pounded with such intensity.

Feeling less than secure holding the handles, I took the plunge and wrapped my hands around his strong chest, placing my cheek against his back as he pulled out onto the street. My blood pulsed almost loud enough to drown out the drone of the engines.

We made a few turns, and in a heartbeat, he'd put both feet back on the ground as he parked on Main Street, just outside his bookstore.

"How was that?"

"It was okay." My rapid breathing was shallow, but the adrenaline coursing through my system was intoxicating.

"Do you want me to grab my truck, or shall I continue? The choice is completely yours. No hard feelings." He twisted to face me.

My hair was flattened, and we were already out and about. "I'm good to go."

He put the bike into gear. "As you wish."

Within no time, we'd picked up speed as we hit the open highway out of Cheshire Bay. All at once I was electrified and filled with raw emotion. I've never felt so safely scared, and I tightened my hold on Adam as a smile spread from cheek to cheek.

# Chapter Sixteen

alfway through the ride, I daringly removed my cheek from Adam's back and gazed over his shoulder. Although it felt so much faster, he was doing the speed limit as we cruised down the highway. I had to admit, the fresh air, while sharp against my face, was highly invigorating, and when we arrived in Moon Bay I'd felt as if I'd been flying and had enough zip whizzing through my body to run a marathon.

Adam parked the bike. "I'll let you off first. But watch that you don't touch the muffler. It'll be super hot."

I wasn't sure how to do this lady-like, but with his feet firmly cemented on the ground, he held the bike firmly while I stood on the pegs. It wasn't as hard to dismount as I expected, and before I knew it, both my feet were on terra-firma. I smoothed out my skirt and undid my jacket.

"How was your first motorbike ride?" Adam kicked out the stand and rested the bike upon it. With ease he undid his helmet and raked his fingers through his hair, looking perfectly polished with so little effort.

I studied the easy way his shoulders relaxed, and the gentle sway about him as he rocked back and forth on his feet.

"That was... Actually, it was a lot of fun." Because the generous smile plastered on my face would've been hard to have denied anything else. I tugged on the chin strap.

Silently, Adam stood closer, and once again his fingers, albeit a little cooler this time, slipped underneath the fastener and eased the strap free.

I took over and pulled the helmet off. "Well, I'm now sporting what they call helmet hair."

After I handed it back to him and hunched down to peer in the side mirror, I fluffed my hair for a little more volume and finger-brushed the tangles out. Surprisingly, I rather enjoyed the less-than-polished look I sported.

Adam stood there watching, as I caught his smirk in the mirror, so I took an extra second or two.

Now that I had made myself presentable, I took in my surroundings. We were on the water's edge, at the marina, where an impressive collection of sailboats and yachts of all sizes were docked. Off the side of a building, stretching out toward the dock, was a massive tent, as big as I'd ever seen, and decorated underneath with thousands of hanging lights. The warm glow to the area gave it a posh appeal, and the cedar trees wrapping around the railings added to the ambiance. If I didn't know better, the centrepieces on the table were greens and candles, something I wanted to inspect further. The whole setup was so beautiful in its simplicity. It took upscale to the next level and definitely upped the *date* factor.

"Breath-taking, isn't it?" However, he wasn't taking in the festival, he was staring right at me.

I broke the gaze and smoothed down my dress. Given the formal wear the other guests wore, I felt wildly undressed.

As if he could read my mind, Adam spoke softly. "You look beautiful."

"Well…"

Before I could say another word, he placed a finger over my lips. "Not another word on that topic."

I nodded and breathed in the crisp salty air. "Can we stroll through there?"

"Already planning for note taking?"

"Of course. Isn't that what this is? A recon of sorts?" Deep in my purse there was a mini notebook and a finely sharpened pencil. I planned on jotting down ideas as discreetly as possible, most likely while in the bathroom.

"Absolutely. But first, we're going to go say hi to an old friend."

A nervous lump settled in the back of my throat. I hadn't been under the impression I was meeting his friends and wasn't sure if I was ready for that.

"Shall we?" Adam offered me the crook of his arm.

Hesitantly, I waited a heartbeat too long to take him up on it.

"I swear, it's a kind, gentlemanly gesture, and nothing more." The sincerity plastered on his face was hard to dispute.

"Okay." And I linked my hand through and rested it on his tight forearm.

"Although I am deeply curious about your other relationships, or maybe it was just one guy, I don't know as I'm not going to ask, but I will say it's a little concerning how you're so untrusting of me."

There wasn't an answer suitable for a reply, so I let the heavy comment weigh down the good mood I was in even though Adam was correct, to a point. It wasn't that I didn't trust him because I'd just ridden on the back of a motorcycle, it was I didn't trust myself to not give off the wrong signals.

Rather than speak, he led us down to the pier and over to the ramp leading to the biggest ship I'd ever set my gaze upon.

From the parking lot, it had looked ginormous but upon closer inspection, it consumed the water's edge, the white hull rising up from the dock like Triton from the sea.

"It's huge."

A smirk filled Adam's face.

"What?" My voice was painted with a smile.

"I just had an overwhelming urge to say *that's what she said* but I stopped myself."

I replayed the previous words and started to laugh. "A big fan of 'The Office', are you?"

"The biggest."

Highly unlikely he could claim that title since I'd watched every episode at least a dozen times, listened to all the podcasts, and knew many behind the scenes moments. If there was a Dundee for Biggest Fan, the award would be mine. In fact, I was the Office Trivia Night champion a few months back.

"Well, I hope you're a better boss than he was."

Adam shrugged. "Michael and I have a lot in common."

"Oh yeah, like what?" I could sense the same kind of humour, but their appearances were much too different as were their personalities.

"I think our main goals are both of love and acceptance, and sometimes that's hard to come by." His voice fell a little, and the tingles in my gut fired up.

Was he being sincere, or just testing the waters with me?

"A little deep for a Saturday night, isn't it?" I nudged him as we stopped at the gangway. My heart skipped a beat, not because of my companion, at least not at this moment, but because I'd never been on a yacht. Not even in my dreams.

"You're absolutely correct. Let's have some fun tonight and scope out the details. I'm sure you can do something like that." With a tip of his head, he pointed back toward the tent, which glowed like a candle in the distance.

There were many factors to consider, but possibly. I'd need a more in-depth look first. "Are we eating there?"

"Absolutely. But first, I need to pick up our tickets. From in there." He pointed to the yacht, standing tall at the end of the dock.

"The owner of the Grand Divertmento has them."

"You know the owners?" My gaze roamed the length of the dock where the yacht was anchored. It was longer than my apartment.

Without a word, he headed to the top of the ramp and paused at the door.

An attractive brunette, tastefully dressed in tall heels, embraced Adam longer than was respectable between friends. They broke apart and she smiled in my direction. "So good to see you again, Adam."

"Thanks, Amber." Adam stepped back and shook the hand of the man beside Amber. His fine clothes and chiseled features screamed wealth and opulence, fitting considering where I stood. "Good to see you again, Antonio."

"Ja, is good to be back."

"I'd like you both to meet Summer." Adam gave me his full attention. "She's a new resident to Cheshire Bay and the CEO of Bayside Markets."

"Welcome to the Bay area, Summer." Amber spoke with such softness I was instantly at ease. "Can I get you some champagne before we head over? We're just clearing up some last-minute changes. Or did you just want the tickets, and we can catch up later?"

I was sure they weren't serving the $10 bottle of Baby Duck, but rather something that cost more than my rent. The urge to sample the good stuff was strong, but Adam was hesitant, and I didn't want to keep him waiting.

"No, I'm fine, thank you."

Adam also shook his head.

Antonio ran his gaze over Adam and linked his hand with Amber's. "You join later when we cast off?"

My gaze jumped from Antonio to Adam, questions running through my mind at lightning speed.

He shrugged and talked like I wasn't a part of the conversation, which was true for the most part. "We may. I promised her I'd show her the festival, but depending on how things go, we'll see later."

"We'll be touring the coast before we return. We leave at nine and would love to have you onboard." Amber spoke in my direction. "It's a gorgeous way to see the island's edge."

It sounded like a plan, albeit a surprise one at that, but really, how often did one get to see their home from the ocean, and from a yacht no less?

"I'll let Summer make the call." Adam looked thoughtfully at me.

I wanted to squeal and blurt out yes as fast as possible, but I took a deep breath to steady myself. "That would be lovely, thank you."

Amber grabbed an envelope off the counter and handed it to Adam. "Your tickets. We'll be there in a bit."

"Are you sitting with us?"

"Of course." Amber smiled and held Antonio's hand. She lowered her voice. "Oh, I just thought I should warn you. She's here tonight."

"Tracy?" The word sailed from his lips, but there was no disguising the vileness.

The head bob was subtle, but it was there. "Originally it was just for the dinner, but you knew that right?"

I searched his face for the answer. Was Tracy his ex? Had to be by the way he tightened up and his eyes narrowed into thin slits.

"Sorry, Adam. A week ago, she bought a ticket for the cruise."

"For one?"

"Two." Amber breathed out the number and reassuringly patted him on the arm. "You'll be good. We'll all be there."

"Who's all?"

I was lost, almost as much as Antonio, who seemed to be looking around at everything rather than the conversation at hand, but I was totally captured by Adam's tight-lipped words. His expression had hardened, and a chill rolled off him.

"Mona and Jesse, and Lily and Eric." She faced Antonio. "I think Eric was coming, right?"

"Ja."

"No Mitch?" Adam questioned.

"No, he and Cedar and the kids are in Seattle."

Adam nodded and cleared his throat. "Well, thanks for the tickets." He tucked the envelope into the inside pocket of his suit jacket. Inhaling, he steadied himself and forced a smile back onto his face. "I want to give her a tour of the area before dinner, so we'll meet you at the table."

"See you soon."

He motioned for me to lead the way, and in silence, we descended the ramp and stepped foot onto the wooden dock.

"You okay?"

Even his steps seemed stiff. "I just need a minute."

"No problem." The urge to break the tension was strong as we walked in a pregnant pause up the ramp and onto the land, but I wasn't sure what to say that didn't sound forced or trite or like cheap small talk. "How do you know Amber?"

"Aside from the fact that Amber has one of the greatest love stories in the Bay area, she and Erin, my sister, all went to school together. Recently, Mona became a part of their gang."

"Oh wow. Everyone really does know everyone else here."

He stopped at an outcropping, where a bench faced the marina. He swept off the seat and motioned for me to sit. "You've heard of the six degrees of separation?"

"That's when you make six connections to another person?" I crossed my legs and took in the captivating view.

Sailboats bobbed in the marina, but it was the lights aboard the big yacht that commanded my attention. And in a couple of hours, I was going for a boat ride on it.

Adam breathed in and out, the whisp of a sigh on his last exhale. "In the Bay area, it's about four degrees of separation, and in Cheshire Bay in particular, it's more like two."

My eyes widened as I faced him. "Wow. Seriously?"

"We're like one giant family."

"Is that good or bad?"

"Depends on who you are." The ugliness seeped back into his tone, and he turned his attention to the docks.

"Did you know your ex was coming to this?"

A deep foghorn sounded in the distance.

"Are you ready to go and have some dinner?" He made to rise, but I softly put my hand on his leg.

"Are you going to answer my question?"

He blew out a puff of air. "I'd heard via the grapevine, but they were only rumours."

The pieces slowly started to click into place. "This really wasn't a special trip to scope out my competition, was it?"

"Depends on how you look at the situation." He shrugged and hung his head a little. "But, truth of the matter, I didn't want to attend alone and have her think she ruined me forever, and oh, shit."

My heart thudded in my chest, and I swallowed down the rising bile. "What?"

"She's coming." He turned his back to a couple walking along the path.

The lady had an air of money surrounding her, her gown was a full-blown princess outfit and if I didn't know better, I swore she had a tiara on. From my distance, she was gorgeous and walked as if she was royalty. Even her date seemed matched to Antonio's level of sophistication, complete with a suit that almost seemed to shimmer under the glow of the port lights. The gentle touches between them, it appeared as if they were in love.

My gaze moved off the happy couple and back to Adam. "So, when you said we were coming to check out the competition, it really wasn't the festival, was it?"

He shook his head and pursed his lips together. "At first it was strictly to help you out. Then, when I heard she was attending, bringing someone like you was a benefit to me. With you on my arm, I could show her–"

I put my hand up to stop him from speaking.

It was happening all over again.

My head swam with bad memories, and I braced myself against the bench.

Adam wasn't one of them, was he? All this time, I thought he'd been different, and liked me for me, not because...

The truth hurt when it hit.

I no longer wanted to be someone's decoration.

An impressive wave of nausea soaked my soul, souring my stomach, and causing sweat to blanket me.

"I'm going to be sick."

"What did I say?"

I jumped off the bench, pounding my way across the grass, and over the concrete paths to the main entrance. I yanked open the door and as I stepped inside, my heart stopped dead.

"Why, look who it is. Hello, Summer."

# Chapter Seventeen

Declan Collins, my former partner at On Demand Specialists, stood at attention in his best navy double-breasted suit, looking as dapper as ever.

"Are you here for the festivities or looking to carve out someone else's heart?" His voice was ice cold, and his demeanour wasn't a degree warmer.

"Summer, wait." Adam entered two steps behind me and had to have felt the sudden rush of a coolness that only two people who hated each other could give off. Adam stopped as if he'd hit an invisible wall.

Declan snapped a nasty glare over at Adam. "Oh, never mind. I see you did find someone new."

The surrounding air chilled another ten degrees, and it froze my feet to the ground.

"What's going on?" Adam flipped his gaze from me to Declan and back to me, where it stayed locked.

"Nothing," I finally managed to whisper.

*How in the hell is Declan here?* On Demand had never branched out beyond the city – there was no need to as clients and potential events were limitless.

Declan's narrowed vision danced between mine with stabbing daggers and over to Adam, where a bemused grin teased his firmly pressed lips. Just watching the corners of his twitching eyes, I was taking an epic level hit and had no weaponry to fight back with.

Unexpectedly, I reached down and fumbled for Adam's hand, a desperate attempt at finding some strength and subtly hinting about the unpleasant situation I—we—were in. His warmth seeped into my numb hand as he tangled his fingers through mine.

While it gave me a boost of stability, it also fed the monster in front of us.

"She's a hooker in disguise, that one. I'd be careful." Declan's hurtful words crushed me.

Adam tensed.

But Declan didn't seem to care, either that or he enjoyed making me uncomfortable, a by-product of our working years. The vitriol was going to spew out like a fountain and considering Adam hadn't walked away and I was rooted in my spot, Declan latched on to his unsuspecting and captive audience. "You owe me money."

"I owe you nothing." The words betrayed my quivering weakness as they came out with more power than I expected. "It's over."

"Are you sure? I never claimed what was rightfully mine."

147

He ran a steely cold gaze up and down my body. "You're such a fucking whore."

Adam pulled his shoulders back and a low growl roared. "Listen, *friend.* I don't know what your problem with Summer is, but I'd advise you to cut it out. *Right. Now.*"

Declan didn't back down. Instead, he laughed and patronisingly patted Adam on the shoulder while he spoke to me. "You got this one wound up quite tight, don't you? Are you lying to him too? Does he know the truth? The real truth?"

Adam erased any distance between him and Declan and curled his fingers into his palm as he raised it.

"Adam, no!" I stepped between them. "He's not worth it."

A security guard appeared out of thin air. "What's going on here, Gentlemen?"

My focus jumped between Adam and Declan, mentally screaming at the two of them to step back and breathe.

Adam took the first retreating move. "Nothing."

Declan did the same, but the smirky scowl never left his face.

I pushed against Adam's chest. His heart pounded relentlessly through his shirt and his breathing was clipped. "C'mon. He's not worth your time. Trust me on this."

He took another step back and then another. Once there was a sizeable distance between the two men, I let out my breath. I hated violence with a passion.

It seemed for the first dozen heartbeats, all eyes followed us. We made our way to the host and got our table assignment, which was thankfully across the hall, near the marina's edge.     Adam was still huffing and muttering under his breath as we approached the table where another couple was already seated. He pulled out my chair, and I collapsed into it.

Reaching across the table, he shook hands, then introduced me. "Jesse, Mona, this is Summer."

Attempting to tuck the unpleasant scene away, I rose, returning the gesture with a polite smile. "Nice to meet you."

Jesse's gaze jumped between us and Declan, who still stood at the entrance to the dining area with his targeted hate aimed at me. "Everything okay?"

Adam faced me and swallowed. It looked like a river of rage boiled under the surface and threatened to erupt. Long gone was the light in his eyes, instead, they were as dark as coal. "I think some explanations are due, but yes, for now, everything's okay."

"Can we go outside for a minute?" I whispered, pivoting my body away from the table and his friends.

Mona pointed to the door off the side of the stage. "There's a private patio that way."

"Thank you." I started moving, but Adam stood still, clutching the back of the chair. "You coming?"

"I'll meet you there."

I had two choices looming in front of me – head to the private patio, wait for Adam, and unload everything about Declan, or storm by Declan with my tail tucked between my legs. Neither was ideal. A giant rogue wave crashing over the edge of the restaurant and sweeping me away, or a freak bolt of lightning striking me down were better options. Much better.

"Fair enough. Excuse me." I gave a small nod to our tablemates and pulled my shoulders back.

The fresh air would do me some good.

Pushing open the patio door, I wrinkled my nose at the smell. It wasn't as salty, nor as fresh as I'd hoped but rather had a tinge of fuel mixed with it, giving it an unpleasant yet tolerant smell. No wonder the patio was private. It didn't even have a great view – just more docks, smaller ones with smaller boats.

I huddled under my jacket, bracing myself as Adam stepped outside. "Who's explaining things first?"

There was still the whole Tracy situation that led to the unpleasant Declan encounter. Why hadn't I just walked to the parking lot? I could've avoided the giant explosion.

He shook his head as he approached me, his voice terse and clipped. "In all my life, I've never raised a hand to anybody. Interrupted a few fights, definitely, but never had the urge to hit a guy the way I want to hit him. Who the hell was that?"

My hands fell to my sides. "Declan."

"An ex, I take it?" Sadly, he kept his distance and leaned against the ledge, his knuckles turning white from the death grip on the railing.

"Actually, no." A cold sweat built across my neck, and I shivered as the ocean air blew over it. "I don't really like to talk about it."

"You owe me something." He turned around and stared at me, his voice as hollow as my heart. "Throw me a bone. Give me a morsel. Anything."

"It's complicated." My stomach churned at the memories, and my mouth went dry. "And I'd really rather not talk about it."

"He's the reason you don't date, right? He has to be."

My eyes widened.

"I'm not stupid, Summer. I could put that together quite easily. What did he do to you?"

My head throbbed and my whole body started aching and growing weak. The air around me chilled like winter and my fingers turned ice cold.

Focus.

I needed something to focus on. I scanned the tables through the windows, to the patrons inside laughing and having fun, to the centerpieces I had wanted a better look at, to the servers in their black penguin suits milling around with trays of drinks.

"Summer?" Adam's voice was far away and hazy, like a foghorn in the thick of the fog.

A metallic scraping sound shattered my thoughts and suddenly cool metal touched the backs of my legs. In slow motion, my vision blurred as the people at the nearby table turned in my direction, their jaws slowly opening, and their eyes widening in horror. My heart beat out a dying rhythm, one painful thump after another.

"Sit."

I complied, and feeling faint, I lowered my head and gripped my knees. "I don't feel so good."

He dragged another chair over and sat in front of me. His hands had chilled too, and I imagined little cool patchy streaks of blue on my thighs as he gave them a rub. "What happened between you and that guy? Do you owe him money?"

I sighed. There was no way I was getting out of this situation without an explanation of the scene that preceded it. "Declan and I were business partners at On Demand."

*Could I just leave it at that?*

A slight scowl penetrated his features. I wasn't off the hook yet.

"Declan was my mentor, a strong leader, and an unscrupulous teacher. Whatever our clients wanted for their events, we made it happen. I'd locate whatever was needed, and Declan was the guy who sealed the deal, and not always ethically." There was a desperation in my tone begging for that explanation to be enough, and I held my breath waiting for Adam to speak or give me a sign of some kind. He barely even blinked. "There were a few cases he thought would help elevate my status within the On Demand world, but since he was my boss, agreeing to be on the file with him came with a cost. These things always did."

Adam sat there stone-faced and rubbed my thigh, to the point I thought I was getting rug burn.

"Do you really want to hear this?" Because I sure as hell didn't want to show who I was to the first guy in years I'd actually had feelings for.

"I think it's best that I do."

I hung my head and felt the shame of the professional life stomp on my shoulders. "At first, it was really no big deal. Innocent really. We'd get concert tickets, and we'd go together. You know, like co-workers. But as his clientele became more and more prestigious, so did the kickbacks. They were usually an exclusive and expensive treat, like a helicopter tour or a trip in the client's personal jet for dinner in San Francisco. In return for lavishly including me on these once-in-a-lifetime perks, there were certain expectations, if you will."

Adam inhaled and removed his hand from my thigh, a reaction I expected but hoped he wouldn't have followed through on.

"You're talking about extortion." His voice was barely audible.

"Partly." More like Declan was my business pimp, and I was his street-walker. He had zero issues loaning me out to date whichever high executive asked.

Adam's breath hitched.

I removed my focus from the concrete patio and rolled it up over Adam's until I met his questioning gaze. "After a while, I learned how to leverage my assets to my advantage, and I made good use of them. Declan's clients were royalty, and I was rewarded accordingly, so in turn I had to repay the favour. However, we were a fierce team and truly lived up to our name – On Demand.

"Then, one night he thought it would look great to our

highest-paid client if we accepted his box seat tickets and he proposed to me in front of a huge crowd. It would give our client great exposure, and it was all in fun. Declan said we could go years before actually needing to go through with a wedding."

"He was thinking long term?"

"Probably, he had events booked years ahead." I shrugged. "As the man about to propose, Declan planned the whole mock event, and I was in on it, but it was just the two of us who knew the truth. At least I thought it was for show, but some warning bells went off prior and as the big moment happened, I couldn't do it. I couldn't even pretend to accept, and he was crushed. Not just because I'd turned the event down, but I'd turned *him* down."

"So, you do have some moral integrity?"

A painful lump crushed the back of my throat, even if Adam's words were truth, they stung. "Maybe a little because I knew by turning him down, I was finished. This was a huge night for him, and I blew it. The people behind us actually booed, which didn't help. I pushed the ring back and left. It was beyond embarrassing."

Adam ran his fingers through his hair as the most painful sound I'd ever heard breezed over his lips.

"Naturally, I expected awkwardness and anger since I hadn't lived up to my end of the bargain, but Declan took it a step further. I had been fired before I'd even got home, he removed my name from our mutually linked client accounts and had already emailed them to inform them how due to circumstances beyond On Demand's control I would no longer be working with them. The next morning, he sent me an itemized bill, through a lawyer, for the costs associated with the staging, and everything else he figured I owed him because he hadn't already taken enough. If I didn't pay up, he said he'd tell everyone and anyone how I slept with him only to rise to the top, and how he was the victim of sexual harassment."

"Let me get this straight. In addition to the extortion, he blackmailed you?"

"He had emails, photographs, everything, and it would've been all too easy for him to have played the victim. I was locked out of On Demand and had access to nothing." I shivered violently knowing my clients also had pictures. "I drained all my savings and gave him everything I had just to keep things quiet. But it gets worse."

"Worse?"

A long, pitiful sigh escaped my lungs, and with it came something deeper than shame. "To this day, Chloe doesn't know what truly happened. She thinks Declan saw more into our professional relationship and that's why he proposed, and there's probably a ribbon of truth to that. Plus, she thinks I quit. I'm too embarrassed to let her know just how awful a person I really am."

"But your trips? The concerts and whatever?"

"She knew about those, but she doesn't know what I gave up for them. Figures they were just a sweet perk." I searched Adam's face, for a flicker of hope that he wouldn't toss me to the side like the used piece of garbage I was. "So, you can see why…"

He blew out a long breath and shifted in his seat. "That's a lot to unpack."

"I know. I never expected to see Declan again. I'm sor–"

His finger covered my lips and his eyes narrowed. "Stop apologizing. Please. I need to think."

I clasped my hands together and scanned the area. People were milling about on the other side of the glass, wrapped in their own enchanting world as they laughed and touched and seemed genuinely happy.

What was supposed to be a pivotal moment in my life, a turn to the positive side, was now filled with despair and anguish. Happiness was not my friend, not when it came to the members of the opposite sex, and neither were relationships. Sadly, Declan was the icing on a cake of relationships. Some cuts just never healed.

# Chapter Eighteen

The air was heavy with unspoken words and silent gestures. Adam huffed and went to speak, but when his mouth opened, the silence was shattering. He hadn't moved and kept a hand on my knee, however he looked everywhere but at me.

I wasn't sure if I should speak, but I was shivering just sitting there. The breeze had picked up and the sweat on the back of my neck was forming into tiny ice crystals.

Adam huffed again, shaking his head, and pulling his hand back. The warm spot on my leg instantly cooled.

"Tell me what you're thinking?" The tone was as timid as my phrasing.

"I don't honestly know."

A fair enough response as I wasn't sure what the right answer would be.

"I think I'll go home. You stay and visit with your friends." I rose abruptly and walked to the door, surprised by my own strength.

"Wait." Adam put his hand on top of mine, sealing us away from the party on the other side. "Just wait."

His shoulders rolled in, and he hunched over as though he carried the weight of the world on his back. For all I knew, he could've been, but he wasn't sharing any of it. "I just don't... I mean, I..."

"I get it."

"What do you get?" His brows knit together, and he tipped his head to the side.

"That it's a lot to digest."

"That it is."

"But I also know I've always been upfront with you."

He snorted. "Ain't that the cold hard truth."

"So, I understand if you don't even want to be friends."

He shook his finger and then placed it on his lips, a deep questioning forming in his eyes. "You see, the thing is..."

I beat him to the punch. "I can't, Adam. I just can't. It goes beyond Declan. He was just the icing on the cake." Adam reached for my hand while his expression softened. "I can't. I honestly believed I could do this, but the moment I finally try, everything blows up in my face. I'm sorry. I'm just not a good person and you deserve someone so much better."

With that, he dropped his hand and I ducked under his arm, opening the door. I sidestepped the table where his friends sat and gave them a weak smile as I headed to the entrance. Declan hadn't moved and must've taken in the whole scene judging by the wide

Cheshire grin on his slimy face.

Before he could say a thing, I walked right by him. I wanted to tell him to fuck right off, and yell and scream, but I took the high road and pushed myself outside into the cool air. Luck was finally on my side, and a cab appeared dropping off a couple of partygoers.

I tipped my head down. "Can you give me a ride?"

"Sure thing, lady."

I hopped in and closed the door, taking a final look back. Adam had followed and now stood beside Declan.


I stared at a spreadsheet full of red numbers and a bank account so overdrawn, it would take years to break even while praying for solutions as I downed my third cup of coffee in total silence.

Last night I'd stayed out too late nursing the one beer I had cash for at Amber's Ale until I figured Chloe had gone to sleep, and tiptoed in, tossing and turning all night long. When I awoke, I cowardly listened until she had left for her three-day trip just so I wouldn't have to face her.

I reviewed my vendor list until I was blue in the face. Adding more wouldn't really help as I still needed to pay for their tables, chairs, and now tents, and increasing that only added to the money pit I was drowning in. The space I'd sold my soul to Satan to rent was thankfully paid until the end of May with vendor fees but was due for a renegotiation of terms at the end of the month. Looking at the numbers though, the business wasn't going to last that long.

I'd screwed up and mismanaged everything.

Offering up my body wouldn't even help. I was up shit creek without a paddle. I had twenty-seven vendors who were counting on me to help their business, and I couldn't let them down. But I didn't know how to help. Clearly, I didn't know the first thing about running a business. It had all been smoke and mirrors. I was a fake, and when they found out, I was completely fucked.

# Chapter Nineteen

Tuesday evening rolled around – my *date* with Kyle. Thank God the two people I cared about the most were otherwise consumed with their jobs and wouldn't know about my indiscretions.

Besides, Adam hadn't returned my phone call, and I assumed he was still trying to process what I revealed about Declan. I hadn't told him everything, but the details were likely best left to the imagination, as he probably couldn't even understand what truly went on behind closed doors. Some things were better left unknowing. Pandora's Box could remain closed.

As per our agreement, I waited for Kyle outside The Grill, a restaurant on the southern tip of the peninsula, almost as far away as you could get from downtown.

I kept my attire simple, a nice sweater and clean jeans, but was a little surprised to see how much nicer Kyle dressed since his dress pants, shirt, and tie were a far cry from the overalls he wore on Saturdays.

I waved and plastered on my smile, remembering my promise to be civil and polite. "Good evening."

The smell greeted me before he did, the air pungent with the repulsive stench of weed.

"Did you drive high?" My eyes grew three sizes at the thought.

"I walked here. I live right down there." He pointed down the road to the bay. The only buildings on that road were motels and not even high-quality ones.

But it was none of my business, although I hadn't planned on spending the next four hours at a restaurant, I sure as hell wasn't driving him anywhere, and I wasn't going back to his place to chill.

"Shall we go in?"

"Give me a few minutes to air out." He pulled a tiny atomizer of what I could only guess was air freshener and spritzed it around him.

*Good plan.* Every car that pulled into the parking lot I studied, making sure it wasn't someone I knew, or more specifically, hoped it wasn't Adam. My gaze darted from the car to the door of the restaurant and all around. Thankfully, no one looked remotely familiar, and in a town this small, that was a small blessing.

"Do I smell better now?" Kyle leaned toward me.

Hesitantly I moved closer to confirm. "Yeah, it's better."

"Lead the way."

As I walked ahead of him, he had the audacity to put his hand on my lower back while we entered the lobby. I stepped off to the side, away from him, and over to the hostess stand.

"For two."

"Right this way."

I made sure to keep some distance between Kyle and me, but just, I still needed to uphold my end of the bargain.

"Oh, not here," Kyle told the hostess as she pointed to a perfectly decent table for four. "What about over there?"

"Of course." She grinned easily and walked us over to a circular booth. There was another booth with a table of four within earshot, so at least we weren't totally secluded.

I slipped into the booth, and he slid in beside me, putting us hip to hip, so I moved around to sit opposite him.

"Where are you going, sweetheart?"

My cringe meter ratcheted up ten notches with the word *sweetheart*. "It's easier if I can face you."

"But I want to sit beside you."

"This will work better this way." I smiled through gritted teeth. Four more hours. I could do it. I'd done worse than this before. "Please."

He opened his suit jacket and pointed at a tri-folded piece of paper. "I needn't remind you, right?"

"The deal was no touching."

He flattened the agreement over the tablecloth. "Actually, the deal was no kissing or sex, so touching is within reason. This is your signature, right?"

I leaned over and grabbed the paper. I had signed in blue, and my signature was in black at the bottom. Somewhere he had the original, this was a photocopy.

"In case you get any ideas. You're mine for the night. You signed."

I scanned over the document, and my jaw hit the floor. In my haste to not have Adam peek at any of the details, I had failed to read it thoroughly. It wasn't official, and probably wouldn't hold water in court, but by signing I had agreed to be his girlfriend for the night, and, despite my objections, that involved touching. If I broke our agreement, I had to find a new rental company, and immediately pay the difference in the discounted tent rentals. Moving forward, he wouldn't even supply tables and chairs, and since he was the only one within a hundred-kilometre radius, I was royally fucked.

"So, what will you be having?"

"Crow pie," I said, hanging my head.

"I figured." A wicked smile crossed his face, and with it, my last shred of dignity shriveled.

The server appeared to take our orders.

"A draft of beer," Kyle started. "Honey, what do you want?"

"You know I'm not feeling great. How about just a glass of water?"

"You can't have water, have a tea or something? Or maybe something alcoholic would relax you, make you feel better?" To anyone else, it looked like a sympathetic grin, but I'd seen that glint in the eyes before along with the twitch of the lips, and there was nothing soothing about it.

"Chamomile tea?" I asked our server, who couldn't have been old enough to understand body language, if he could even legally serve Kyle's alcohol.

"Sure thing."

"C'mon, you promised you'd be good." The hint of a whine in his voice curdled my blood.

I knew exactly how this night was going to go, and I hated myself for having even asked about getting a better deal. Should've just sucked it up and not inquired to begin with. Why was hindsight always better?

I swallowed down the bitter lump and pulled from my mental pocket a list of small talk questions. "Have you been here before?"

"Several times. The food is good." He reached across the table and grabbed my hand, stroking it with one hand while the other held it firmly in his grasp. "You know, you really don't look so good."

"I really don't feel so good."

"Are you nervous about our date?"

My heart hammered hard enough that I was sure he knew the answer, but I didn't want him to have any more advantage than he already had. "No, not at all. I think my salad at lunch was made with questionable meat."

He slipped on over to my side of the booth, and it was either move away and fall on to the floor, or grin and bare it. His arm slinked around behind my back and pulled me close before I had a chance to escape. "You'll see I'm not a monster. I'm actually a nice guy when you get to know me, just give me a chance."

Suddenly I understood why he had to buy a date. Only monsters tried to convince their prey how decent they were.

Our drinks arrived, and I was grateful for the interruption.

"Tell me about your specials." I wanted our server to stay as long as possible.

"Just the pasta bowl."

His quick four words killed my hope.

"Do you have chicken noodle soup?"

"We have chicken fingers."

"No, thanks." I didn't want anything heavy in my stomach.

"We'll both have the specials." Kyle grabbed my menu and handed it to our server. "And minimal interruptions, please."

His hand settled on my lap and my breathing caught in my throat as it threatened to strangle me from the inside out. "Relax. You're just playing the part of my girlfriend, and that's all. Just relax."

My skin tingled. Sweat built between my shoulder blades, and there was an unmistakable hint of body odor, although I was sure it came from me. I crossed my legs, and in doing so, managed to push his hand higher up my thigh.

"Please, stop." My voice threatened to crack, and if it did, I knew I was in deep trouble. Instead, I found a little bit of courage and managed to give my voice more strength than I thought I could.

He lifted his hand but set it back on top of my knee.

"Thank you." I swallowed a sip of my tea. "Why don't you

tell me about how you got into the rental business?"

"You're interested in that?"

I feigned wild-eye delight. "Why wouldn't I be? We're both business owners, it's interesting to see how you started."

That topic managed to open him up and allowed me to act the part of a doting girlfriend who bobbed her head at all the right times while zoning out a little. It was obvious he loved to talk about himself, and over the course of his beer, our dinner, and even a small dessert, he talked pretty much non-stop. As the conversation carried on, he even managed to put a little breathing room between us.

It was the relief I needed to loosen up. Once there was a little distance between us, I started to relax and for a heartbeat, I actually listened to one of his stories. It ended with a terribly off-colour joke, but his delivery was so funny, I laughed. A genuine, earnest laugh with my head tipped back.

However, the moment was short lived.

As I glanced around the restaurant, I spotted him - Adam. Sitting with another lady and a young child between them. The worst though wasn't that he was out on a date with someone, it was how I interpreted his narrowed eye gaze, which volleyed between me and Kyle. My date. Who was currently rubbing my hand as if we'd been together for years and not a couple of hours.

# Chapter Twenty

I broke eye contact with Adam and swore a blue streak inside my head that would put a sailor to shame. If I had wanted anything to happen between us, it was null and void now. Who knew what was running through his head as he stared at me *on a date*, the very thing I told him I didn't do? Even though I knew what was happening between Kyle and I was strictly a business deal, and a sick one at that, I also knew it did not look like that to the outside world.

Horrified wouldn't even begin to explain the multitude of emotions swirling through me. Adam sat at the table, staring at me, despite the little girl constantly tugging on his sleeve. I couldn't bear to see the hurt yet confused expression flicker on and off his face, so I turned back to Kyle, who was yammering on about some baseball game.

"Hey, I think I'd like to leave."

"And where would you like to go?" A sly grin stretched from ear to ear as he stroked my hand.

"I think I'd like to stretch my legs, maybe walk off this heavy meal." I flagged our server over. "The cheque please."

"There's a nice walking trail out to the lighthouse."

In my sound mind, there was no way I'd take a walk on a dark path—alone—with this guy. Even if I were three sheets to the wind, I'd have enough common sense to know that was not a safe option.

"Actually, I didn't wear the proper shoes for walking. Maybe we could do some shopping or something?"

Main Street was littered with little eclectic shops.

"This isn't a big city, sweetheart. Most stores closed hours ago."

Right. Also, all the hidden gems Adam had shown me were of a less public variety. "What are some neat things we can do here? I'm sure I haven't seen everything."

"Oh, you definitely haven't seen everything." He wiggled his brows, and I fought the urge to throw up.

From the corner of my eye, I watched as Adam rose from his table and avoided passing in front of mine. I took it to be a sign to get the hell out of the restaurant.

"You know what, let's discuss it outside. I need a breath of fresh air." I stretched my neck a little to look overtop the booth, in a desperately pitiful attempt to locate Adam. He had disappeared.

"Alright, alright." It sounded very Matthew McConaughey-like; too bad it didn't have the same appeal coming from Kyle.

I pulled some cash from my wallet and set it on top of the bill, but Kyle pushed it back toward me.

"I'll get it this time; you can get it next time."

I lowered my voice. "There won't be a next time. Remember? This was a one-time deal."

"And after May long weekend? The temperatures start to climb. Believe me, you'll want what I have to offer." His tongue flicked across his lips like the snake he was. "Admit it, you'll be with me for a while. A nice long while."

At least I knew I was covered until the long weekend. My top priority tomorrow morning was to expand my search for another rental person.

As much as I would've enjoyed keeping the cash, and having some on hand, I didn't need anything else hanging over my head. I left my portion on the bill.

Kyle added his own money to the pile and gestured for me to leave. I hopped out first, and Kyle was quickly on my heels. Hopefully, we could make it to the front door before spotting Adam and making a truly horrible night even worse.

"Shit, I forgot something. Meet you at the front." Kyle spun around, and I had a moment to breathe. Finally.

But Lady Luck enjoyed kicking a person when they were down.

Just as I reached the hostess podium, Adam appeared from the restroom hallway, and he stopped dead when he saw me.

"Having fun tonight?"

I really wasn't and implored Adam to sense my uncomfortableness with my rolled-in shoulders and sour expression.

"It's not what you think."

"Oh really? Because it looks like you're out on a date. Guess now that you've broken the fear with me, things have changed." The river of hurt was strong, and the current threatened to take me out.

"Honestly, it's not what you think. Please believe that." I poured emotion into my voice, a begging sound, oozed with desperation for him to not believe what he was seeing.

Before I could expand and answer his questionable expression, Kyle slithered right behind me, his hand settling on the small of my back. "Should we get going, sweetheart?"

Adam rocked back on his feet and his left eyebrow nearly jumped into his hairline. "Not what I think, eh?"

Kyle pushed against my back, urging me to go, which only fueled the anger roaring deep inside.

"Yeah, well, you're out with someone." If I had been a child, no doubt I would've stuck out my tongue too.

"My sister and niece, but thanks. Thanks for thinking that about me after…" He shot daggers at Kyle. "Well, you know."

"This has been as awkward as all get out. If you'll excuse me, my girlfriend and I were just leaving." Kyle grabbed my hand, tugging me toward the door.

With each yank, pieces of my heart were scattered on the ground. All I had to do was ask Adam for help. Instead, pride, stupid foolish pride, and a giant sense of what scene would be created if I said a thing came into play.

Kyle was no fool, and my previous experiences knew that. I

had to be subtle. And Adam had to pick up on that.

"You're so wrong about this." My final desperate words to Adam were said under my breath before I was pulled into the parking lot, where the crisp cool air smacked against my heated cheeks and chest. Just when I started to think there was a possibility of something more with Adam, Murphy and His Damn Law came into play.

"Where should we go?" Kyle asked as people walked by.

"To hell."

"Hey, I'm offended."

Since my end of the bargain had still not been fulfilled and there were still a couple of hours remaining, Hell actually seemed like a viable option especially since I was already halfway there.

Shaking my head, I asked, "So, what should we do?"

Kyle snorted. "There's not really much to do in this po-dunk town. You won't go for a walk, there's no shopping to be done. We could go back to my place—"

"No, thank you."

"You didn't need to be so quick to turn me down."

"Was there a part in our little agreement where it said I had to be a fucking pushover? I stated from the get-go there was to be no sex, and your constant insinuations at the night ending with it is starting to get on my nerves."

"Geez, lady. Take it down a notch."

Passersby stopped to take in the conversation, and for the first time, I didn't care. I was angry, tired, and far beyond humiliated to give two shits. Their stares somehow fed my courage.

"Take it down a notch? Really. All evening long you've been invading my personal space, all so I can save a few hundred dollars a week, and you know what? It's not worth it."

"And all evening long I've been trying to show you a good time, and at one point, you even laughed, so don't tell me you haven't at least enjoyed yourself a little." His voice rose and the anger coursing through it was unmistakable.

But I didn't care. I was on a roll. "Yes, when you stopped being so you. Once you started to back off, yes, you were a decent guy, but you're still someone who is grossly misguided in what a woman wants. Show a little respect."

"I'll show you respect." He raised his hand but stopped and scratched the back of his head when a couple of guests moved in closer. "Just a little disagreement, people. Nothing to see here."

I thought otherwise and figured they could camp out in my car if they wanted.

He glanced around at the small crowd forming, and inhaled sharply, his nostrils flaring slightly. "After tonight, we're square, okay?"

"I'll get a break on the tent pricing?"

"Until May long, as I agreed. After that, it's full price, but you have to finish off the evening so why don't we head to the bar? You can dance away this angry vibe you're giving off."

It was surprisingly a great idea – there'd be plenty of people as it was definitely a public venue, but I tried to act aloof as I calmed my nerves.

"Sure. I like dancing. It'll be quieter since it's still early in the evening, and a weeknight."

"Do you mind driving?" He got closer, and I moved my head back. "I had a beer tonight and don't want to get another DUI. Besides, it's not far."

I didn't want to be in a tightly confined space with him, especially after the little heated exchange, and even more so because warning bells were going off loud and clear. "You could walk. I heard there's a bridge that connects this section to the bar section."

"Then come with me." He extended a hand.

I inhaled and forced a smile. "It's best if I drive and meet you there."

Slowly, the lingering people entered the restaurant, once again leaving us to ourselves.

"I think you driving is a great idea." He grabbed my wrist and an angry snarl curled up the side of his lips. "Get in the fucking car."

"No." My voice was firm but not as much as my stance.

From the depths of his pocket, he pulled out a table knife as he yanked me close. "I said get in the god-damn car."

My heart hammered in my chest and now I wished I had told Chloe what was going on and been more upfront with Adam.

"Which one is yours?" He held me close as we walked by each vehicle.

"That one." My voice shook, and I was slowly losing feeling in my legs with fear.

"Get in, and any funny business, and you'll be wearing this.

Give me your keys." He waved the silverware as I slipped into the driver's seat. "Buckle up."

I did as he said while surges of adrenaline wracked my body. He remotely locked the doors as he ran around to the passenger seat, only unlocking them to slide in beside me.

He started the car. "Now drive."

"Where to?"

"Just until I tell you not to." He placed his hand on my thigh.

"Stop." My firmest voice grew.

He rubbed his fingers along my inner leg as I pushed on the accelerator, moving us away from the sanctity of the Grill.

My pulse pounded in terror, and my heart beat like a thunderstorm.

"You embarrassed me in public, and now you're going to pay, and I'm going to enjoy collecting it." His hand moved from my leg to my cheek, where he stroked down over the side of my neck and across my breast.

I screamed.

A horn blasted and a set of headlights flashed.

In that split second, a moment of brilliance hit.

I yanked the steering wheel to narrowly avoid hitting the car, but I stepped on the gas instead of the brake and drove straight into a solid tree. The airbag exploded and darkness welcomed me.

As I came to, voices surrounded me. Twisting my neck, and blinking through a whopper of a headache, I noted the passenger door was open. The bastard ran away.

# Chapter Twenty-One

With Kyle nowhere to be found, and the car, which was a total write-off, I wound up sitting in the police station, preparing to give a statement to the officer. Just as I was about to go in, Chloe marched in through the double glass doors.

She wasted no time in crossing the waiting room to stand before me, concern etched on her face. "I heard from an EMT you were treated at the scene of an accident, but it wasn't really an accident according to the eyewitnesses, and they were bringing you here. Are you okay?"

"Minor bruises from the airbag, just damage to my pride and soul."

"What the hell happened? There's rumours you purposely drove into a tree." Her voice nearly shrieked, and I had to grip her arms to settle her down.

"You wouldn't believe me if I told you."

She reached out and wrapped me in a hug, and for a moment,

all felt right in the world. Mostly. Aside from the fact how Adam probably hated me and never wanted to talk to me again. How my car was totalled, and now I wouldn't have the cash needed to start paying off my debts. And Kyle was out on the lam. But at least in Chloe's embrace, I had a moment of peace.

It was to be short-lived.

"Miss Bates, Officer Forsythe will take your statement."

"I won't be long." I looked long and hard at my best friend, wondering if she was going to badger the officer currently sitting at the desk and pepper him with questions.

"Maybe I should come, hear the story so you don't have to repeat it, and be there for moral support. You need me. You look like you need a friend." She cupped my cheek, and I melted into it, savouring the moment.

I knew once the truth came out, things were going to change. It was undeniable.

"I don't know if you want to hear this."

She patted my arm. "I've got your back."

"Promise not to hate me?"

Chloe furrowed her brow, and concern washed over her. "Why would I hate you?"

"Miss Bates?" The officer behind the counter chirped. "Officer Forsythe is waiting."

With the weight of the world on my shoulders, I lumbered to the side door the officer pointed to and walked down a long corridor with Chloe steps behind. Unlike the tv shows where you get placed into a sterile room with mirrors, this was more like an office with carpeting, artwork, padded chairs and armrests, a nice laminate desk, and a noticeable absence of a giant wall mirror.

Officer Forsythe waved for us to sit. Her hair was in two tightly woven braids that surrendered to her manipulation, and I doubted there was a sympathetic bone in her body. She sat ramrod straight behind the desk and pulled an official piece of paper and a pen from the drawer.

"I'm going to write down the details to help us form a proper statement. Why don't you start at the beginning?"

"How far back do you want me to go?" I didn't even have an ounce of humour in my tone, but if I did, it would've been lost.

She stared me down, total seriousness crusting her already hardened features.

I turned away from her and faced Chloe. "I really don't think you want to hear this. It's going to hurt so much."

"I know you're scared, but I'm here for you."

"Please remember that when we're done." My voice cracked.

Like the officer was my priest, I unfolded on them both.

About everything.

About Declan, and his scrupulous dealings, and as Adam put it, the extortion and blackmailing issues. Then I launched into how broke I was and because I had screwed my credit over with each add-on, I couldn't secure a bank loan, so my startup was killing me, and that's why I reached out to Kyle. I ended my total confession with the declaration of how I purposely smashed my car into the tree, knowing full well insurance wasn't going to cover it, and that the money was gone, but at least Kyle couldn't take me to a secondary location.

Although I felt like a weight had been lifted, as I took in the stunned expression on the officer's face and the *what-did-I-just-hear* look on Chloe's, the heaviness just pressed back between my shoulder blades.

"You're broke?" She asked, her tone one of indignation.

"Flat broke."

"And you couldn't tell me?"

"I didn't know how." I felt like razor-thin glass, one tiny misstep and I was going to shatter into a million pieces.

"And Declan? Really? I thought he'd fallen for you, and that you two would've made a cute couple. I thought his proposal was real?" She shook her head, and a strand of blond hair escaped her ponytail. "All this time, Declan had been using you? Extortion and blackmail? Seriously?" She blinked rapidly. "And Adam knew this before me? You trusted him before you trusted me?"

"I'm sorry."

She blew her breath out, and it was like a mini windstorm as it sailed by.

My words started tripping over themselves. "I was failing. Do you know how hard it is, what that feels like to know you're the total opposite of what success is? I didn't plan on ever seeing Declan again, and when it happened, I really felt like there was no choice. I had to tell Adam. If it helps, he nearly punched out Declan."

She bounced her leg, and if it was in rhythm with her heart, it was beating fast.

I, on the other hand, was starting to feel better, amazingly enough.

Chloe sighed again and shook her head. "So, if I'm following this correctly, after everything you've overcome to finally admit you'd want to date Adam, he saw you out with Kyle?"

"Yes."

It was awful. The pain on his face. I'd betrayed him and I'd be lucky if he even sold me a book. Most likely kick me out of his store.

My cracks were splintering. "I know in my heart, I want to be with him, but I don't know how to win him back. I need your help."

Her long, exasperated sign punctured the air. "I don't even know you anymore. I wouldn't know how to begin to help you."

Officer Forsythe was unreadable, which was scary, but her pen hadn't stopped scrawling across multiple sheets of paper throughout my statement, and the less-than-private conversation between Chloe and me.

Chloe rose abruptly and headed to the door.

"Please don't leave."

"I need time to think, Summer. This is... you're not... I just can't with you right now." Her hand was on the handle, and she was looking anywhere but at me.

A tear escaped her left eye and trailed down her cheek.

"Chloe, please." I whispered, my heart shattering into billions of pieces.

"For what it's worth, I'm really thankful Kyle didn't hurt you. I love you too much to see you hurting, and how I wished you loved and respected me the same. You know what? I need some distance from you right now. To process everything you've just unloaded. I'm sorry."

"Chloe, please."

She avoided me. "You can stay at the apartment, but I won't be."

It was over. I had ruined us but not trusting her with my deepest secrets. "No. You stay. It's your place. Give me an hour."

"One hour." With that, she exited the room, clicking the door closed and furthering our separation.

# Chapter Twenty-Two

I n a heavy fog, with a blinding headache, I left the police station with a copy of my statement, a strong encouragement to reach out to a lawyer with regards to Declan, and the eminent warrant put out for Kyle's arrest, which would further a need for a lawyer.

I suspected Chloe was angry at my behaviour and needed space, and I didn't want to ruffle any more feathers, so I went to our quiet apartment with a weak goal. Pack a few things, get through the market, since I didn't have the money available to refund the vendors, and give her time to assess. With my suitcase stuffed, a blanket from my bed, and a few plastic bags to shelter me from the elements, I wandered around town in the thick of the night, desperate to find a place to sleep for a few hours.

Under a blackened sky, on an edge of a beach near Amber's Ale, I wrapped myself under a blanket and ripped a hole in the seam of a plastic bag, pulling it over my head like a poncho. Amazingly enough, it worked and kept me reasonably warm.

The morning kiss of the sun gently brightened the skies, but it was a poke from a finger that jostled me more.

"Hey, you can't sleep here."

Her voice was warm and soft, and as I blinked to focus, I stared into a vaguely familiar face.

"I'll be moving on." I unfurled my hands from around my belongings and stretched.

"Hey, don't I know you?" She narrowed her eyes and studied me.

I hardly doubt I looked recognizable. The last time she saw me I was way more put together. It was at the regatta, and she was the lady on the giant super yacht, a friend of Adam's.

"You're Summer, right? Adam's girlf–"

I shook my head. "You're correct. I'm Summer."

She scanned the beach. "Did you sleep here overnight?"

There was no point in lying. "Yep. I..." I turned away and slowly lumbered to my feet. "I didn't know where to go."

"Well, you can't sleep on the beach. It's illegal."

"Maybe they'll throw me in jail. At least I'll be warm and fed and have a roof over my head." It was said under my breath. She wasn't supposed to hear, and she wasn't supposed to get a piteous look on her face.

"C'mon. I have something for you."

"For me?"

"Yeah. We've all been down on our luck at one point in our lives. C'mon." This practical stranger, whose name I wanted to say was Amber, reached for my suitcase.

I dusted myself off and pulled the garbage bag off over my head.

Amber gestured for me to follow her out from the edge of her bar patio where I'd sheltered, up the stairs, and into the pub. Once we were inside, a bubbly young lady bounced into the pub.

"Iris, can you get Summer a cup of coffee please, and put some bread in the toaster." Amber set my bag down by the bar.

"Oh no, you don't need to." I waved my hands frantically.

"Please, I insist. And give me a minute to make a phone call. In the meantime, set your things by the door."

I reached for her arm, grabbing it before she got too far. "Please don't call Adam."

Her head tipped to the side.

"I need to fix that on my own."

"It's okay." She patted my arm. "I'll be right back." She turned to the young lady pouring a mug full of steaming coffee. "Iris, please make sure she eats and drinks." With a wink, she disappeared into the back.

Under Iris's watchful gaze, I sat at the bar and picked at the toast, even though it was delicious, and sipped on the coffee, feeling its warmth as it slid down my throat.

A few minutes later, two guests walked into the pub. I also recognized them from the regatta.

Amber walked over and spoke in hushed tones before they came over and sat beside me on the bar stools. Suddenly, I felt like I was the target of an intervention.

"Summer, this is Mona and Jesse."

"Right. We met at the regatta." My gaze fell to the shredded piece of toast.

"Sorry we didn't have a chance to talk much that night." Mona sat on my right, shifting onto the padded seat. "Anyway, Amber tells us you're in a bit of a pickle and we can help."

I lifted my gaze and flipped it between her, Jesse, who stood beside her, and Amber, who looked poised as if to wrap me in a hug should the need arise. Who were these people?

Mona crossed her legs. "My sister has a B&B that's not being used. It would give you temporary shelter, and we'll stock the fridge for you too."

Blinking, because it had to be a dream, I stared. "But you don't even know me, why would you do that?"

Jesse spoke up as he shifted on his feet. He kept a measurable distance from me, preferring to tuck in behind his girlfriend. "We've all been there. If it wasn't for Mona…" He trailed off and shook his head. "Well, she stocked my fridge a couple of times."

"And Jesse gave me shelter when I needed it most."

These two were clearly in love, as there were shared smiles and twinkles in their eyes as they recalled their past.

"We want to help." Mona's smile lit her up from the inside out.

I didn't know her at all, but I sensed her kindness had no boundaries.

"But I have no money, I can't afford it, and there's no way right now I can even think about paying you back. Point me toward a food bank or the nearest homeless shelter or something."

"Summer, it's a gift. Someday you'll be able to pay it forward." She said it like it was the truth, and in the moment, I envied her rose-coloured version of the future; one I couldn't possibly imagine.

"I don't know what to say." I looked them each in the eye, tears threatening, but I fought them hard to stay put.

"Just say okay."

I nodded. "Okay, thank you."

A half-hour later, I was holding the keys to a beautiful bed and breakfast which overlooked the beach. This place should not be empty, and I vowed that if I could maintain the market and not completely hit rock bottom, I'd make sure to showcase this beauty and help to drive customers to it. But for now, I needed to focus on making it to Saturday.


First things first, after a hot shower to wash away the horrible Tuesday evening with Kyle, the police station, and the night on the beach, I sat in front of my computer and drafted an email to my vendors.

Put simply, I was pausing the market for one week to locate

a new rental company as the current one had gone belly up. It wasn't the truth, but I knew there was no way Kyle was going to show his face and live up to the end of his bargain, even without the tents. I still needed tables and chairs. That ship had sailed when he put a knife to my chest.

With that heartbreaking decision made, I scoured the internet for the new changes needed to start turning my life around.

A new rental company.

A debt consolidation company.

A top-notch lawyer who billed after the fact. I needed to go after Kyle, and possibly Declan.

Exhausted from the two days of talking to more companies than I ever imagined, I left the safe sanctity of the B&B and walked downtown. Armed with a little courage, I had to start mending all the broken fences I had destroyed.

First up, was my best friend. I knew she was angry as she hadn't returned my calls, so I booked an appointment at the clinic. For a broken heart.

# Chapter Twenty-Three

Feeling two feet tall, I stumbled into the clinic, and gave my name to the receptionist who was definitely not Darla. Chloe had found a replacement as this lady was new, and thankfully as such, didn't know I knew the doctor personally. The nurse, however, did.

"Please don't tell her it's me," I whispered as Melissa walked me to a back exam room.

She opened the folder as we entered the room, setting it on the small counter. "You're here because you're having chest pain?"

I nodded. It was a dull ache in the centre of my chest.

"Perhaps you should head to the ER in Stewart."

"It's not a heart attack. More like anxiety."

It had to have been hard to stand there, take me in looking like the hot mess I was, and not have any judgment showing. Rather, she nodded in a quick assessment and scratched some notes on a piece of paper. "Dr. Tarkin will be right in."

Alone again, I sat on the crinkly papered exam bed, my heart pounding in the depths of my stomach. Prior to this morning, I didn't think my heart could relocate.

I barely had time to ponder what that meant when a knock occurred, and the door opened. Chloe took one look at me and backtracked.

"Please, Dr. Tarkin, I need to see you."

"This is for patients only." She addressed me like I was a child.

Oh boy, did I have my work cut out for me. "That's what I'm here for. I'm a patient."

"I don't see people I know, it's an ethics thing. You know, the ones you kept hammering on about as far as Justin was concerned." Her arms were crossed tightly in front of her chest.

My ankles linked together as I dangled them. "But I need a doctor. I need you."

She sighed, closed the door, and logged in to the computer. "What's troubling you?"

"I'm having these chest pains." I placed my hand over where my heart used to be.

Her face went serious, and she stepped over to me, unwrapping the stethoscope from around her neck. Instantly, she placed it on my back. "Inhale. Exhale. Slowly." She was methodical, listening to my breathing from different points. "Strong heartbeat. No arrhythmias."

"Really?" I lowered my head, not wanting to see the look in her eyes. "It feels like it's broken."

With that, she straightened out. "Summer, I don't have time for this. I have a full case load today."

"I know, but I booked an appointment, and I have ten minutes. Nine, actually." I pulled my shoulders back. "You won't talk to me, and it's really starting to affect my health." A stabbing pain shot across my chest and my breath caught. "I am so sorry. Really. About everything. I was so embarrassed by what Declan and I were doing. Can you imagine selling out like that? I couldn't tell anyone. Everything was on the line, it was a stupid gamble, and wouldn't you know it, I lost it all. Not my proudest moment."

She looped her stethoscope around her neck and crossed her arms. "Since we've met, I've never kept anything from you, and liars are the lowest of lows."

"I know." An elephant stomped on my shoulders, pushing them closer to my knees. "I'm not proud of what I've done, but I'm trying to fix things. I've contacted a debt consolidation company."

She nodded. "That's a smart start."

I inhaled, daring myself to make eye contact. To show her I'm working on changing, for the better. "And I've secured a job to pay the bills. Actual paycheques every two weeks."

"Doing?" Her perfectly shaped eyebrow settled below her hairline, and her dark eyes narrowed, however, she took in my every word.

"Janitorial work."

There was no shame in it. The hours were perfect – a few evenings a week and all supplies were included. I was in charge of a couple of office buildings, one of which included Mona's. She really had gone overboard in helping me, and I owed her more than she'd ever know.

"Think of it as figuratively and literally cleaning up my life."

"I'm glad you're getting your priorities straightened out." Her features were softening.

A lump formed in the back of my throat which was nearly impossible to swallow as it felt like it had little knives embedded, scratching its way down. "I also contacted a lawyer. To go after Kyle."

She sat on the chair with a slump. Her anger was diminishing, and replacing it was the very best friend I'd ever had with her strength and compassion.

"I was so scared, Chloe. All those talks in college about secondary locations. I knew if he got me there..." My tears broke free, and I buried my face in my hands. "When he touched me... I was terrified. It was me or the car."

"You made a smart decision." Suddenly, her arms wrapped around me, and she tightened her grip. If I didn't know better, I thought she was crying too. "I'm so sorry. That was such an awful night." She ran a hand down the back of my head. "You needed me, and I was so absorbed in all the things you did wrong and my own personal problems that I didn't really listen to the terror you'd just gone through."

"You were upset." I sniffed.

"Very much so, but I shouldn't have taken it out on you." Her embrace tightened. "You never came home."

"I said I wasn't. I was going to wait to see if we go better before I even dared ask."

She sighed and pulled backed, wiping under her eyes. "I know. I went looking for you. Where did you go?"

"I'm holed up at a little B&B that a friend of a friend of a sister owns. Or something like that." I shook my head, trying to remember how it was all connected.

"Oh, Summer. I'm so sorry. Can you ever forgive me?"

Swiping away my own river of tears, I stared into her face. "I came here to ask *you* for that. I was never mad at you. I deserved everything that happened to me."

"No one deserves to be raped."

That one awful word destroyed me, and I openly broke, rivers of hot, angry tears flooding in currents down my cheeks. I started shaking, and a burst of adrenaline soaked my body with sweat.

"We'll get through this. I promise."

"Promise?" I could barely make out her blurry, weak smile.

She tipped her forehead to mine. "We're best friends, right? It's what we swore to do."

"I'm so sorry I damaged the trust between us. I promise no more secrets." I crossed my fingers over my heart.

"No more." It was a statement; firm and unyielding.

"What can I do to make it better? What can I do to fix us?" At this point, if she asked me to grovel at her feet and follow her around town on my knees for a month, I'd agree in a heartbeat.

"Let's discuss it. Over dinner." She paused and wiped under her eyes. "Please come home."

I hopped off the exam table and hugged her. "Are you sure?"

"I wouldn't have asked if I wasn't."

"Oh, Chloe, thank you." I kissed her cheek and hugged her again.

"But seriously, you're medically okay?" She blew her nose and then doused her hands in antibacterial gel.

"I have a lot of anxiety, but it's manageable."

"We can get you some counselling. You're likely past due anyway based on everything that happened with Declan, and On Demand." She scribbled on a notepad, tearing it off and handing it to me. "Do you need a prescription for the anxiety?"

I shook my head. "No, not yet. I think once I deal with a few more important things, it will get better."

"One thing at a time. One day at a time." She stood at the door; my folder tucked under her arm. "I'll be home after five."

"Thank you. You don't know what this means to me."

The smile I'd been waiting for appeared, and it brightened her complexion. "Maybe I do."

After missing the week at the market, it filled my soul with sunshine to be back at it. The new rental company arrived, albeit a little late, but they also came with a full assembly team. The market was set up with tables, chairs, *and* tents within thirty minutes. The wow factor was huge and was worth the slight uptick in cost. Bayside Markets was back in business.

Adam wasn't there when set up was completed, and he didn't show up until thirty minutes before opening. Guess he was keeping his distance from me as much as possible. But I missed his smile. His presence. The way he always managed to show up at the perfect time and have just the right thing to say.

God, I missed everything about him.

Erin was another case altogether, and the glares she sent in my direction as I made my way around taking pictures for Bayside Market's social media pages were worse than what Declan had pierced me with two weeks ago. I was terrified to stop at her setup but had to do it. At that moment, she was the lesser of two evils.

I lifted my phone and swallowed down the rising panic. I wasn't going to avoid her, like a coward would, and like how I desperately wanted to.

"What piece would you like to showcase today?" A lump of shame sat lodged in the back of my throat.

Onto the table, she lifted an 18" high wood carving of a lady on her knees in a dress, hunched over something in her lap. The shoulders caved in, and the back was in a deep roll. Thick strands of wooden hair shielded her face. Rounded hands wrapped across her ample chest. I couldn't make out the package on the lap, but the overall feeling from the carving was one of resounding heartbreak. There was no expression on the carving's face, but somehow it was clear this wooden lady was grieving something.

"It's breathtaking and tragic," I told Erin, unable to take my eyes off it for long.

"Thanks, the idea just hit me, and I had to run with it." She ran her hand down the back, almost as if dusting it off.

"Must've taken you forever."

"Once I hit a groove, it felt effortless."

"It's truly magnificent." Almost a piece I'd like in my living room, although, it would probably envelop me in sadness every time I looked at it. "Ready?"

Erin put her weight onto her right leg, plopping her left in front of her. She stood there, forcing a smile; the kind that never reaches the eyes. "Ready."

I stepped back to make sure I got her, the carving, and her banner into the frame. "Thank you."

She stepped closer, and I held my ground. No way was I getting too close.

"He's hurting, you know. Seeing you with that other guy destroyed him. You should've been upfront with him."

"Looks can be deceiving. There was absolutely nothing romantic between that guy and me."

"I saw it with my own eyes." Her own raised as if to call me on a bluff.

"And it was all an act. You have to believe me." I inhaled sharply as the chest pain sparked and a nasty shudder coursed through me from top to bottom. It hurt to inhale, and a familiar, but unwelcome, stabbing pinprick of pain circled my chest. Instinctively,

I covered my heart and let out a gasp. After a moment, it passed. "Did you not hear about the accident in the parking lot?"

My focus went back to the carving, to stare at what was etched into the lap.

"That was you?"

I nodded and gave a weak smile, my go-to rather than a storm of tears. "That date, it was an act. A nightmare, really."

"Well, someone believed your act was Academy Award worthy because he's gone and done something stupid because of it. Twice now."

Slowly, I turned and scoped out Adam's tent. Standing beside him, laughing, and leaning against his arm was a pretty blonde, who obviously spent a lot of time preparing to leave the house. Her hair was perfect, and the sweet little outfit she wore fit with the amount of makeup plastered on her face. But it wasn't her captivating appearance commanding my attention, it was the total opposite look from Adam. Along with a forlorn expression, and his hair hanging in his face, his right hand peeked out from a sling, completely wrapped in bandages.

Little flares of unrest settled in my gut.

Adam spotted me and held that connection, sending a flurry of butterflies soaring. But it was brief. Too brief. As if he was embarrassed, crimson blanketed his cheeks as he abruptly turned away.

A million thoughts scrambled through my brain, not one of them making much sense.

Did he think I wouldn't notice his hand? Eventually, I was going to have to show up at his table and take his picture.

Erin full out snorted and carried on as if I hadn't completely zoned out. "What a freaking nasty bitch. He deserves better."

Still, what could I do about it? I had no plan to win him back. Everything and anything I'd conceived over the past ten days was corny and cliché. But seeing him with the sophisticated blonde, it cemented how he'd moved on, and why he hadn't returned any of my phone calls or texts. Deep down, I knew she was a better fit for him, and obviously, he did too.

There was no way I could make him happy. I hadn't even managed that for a couple of hours. We had an hour max on regatta Saturday. One hour of total and true happiness.

*Oh, shit.*

With that realisation, my stomach hardened, and a burning sensation pooled around my chest. That one hour of happiness was the best I'd had in the last seven years and now it was gone. I'd never get it back. Not even if I truly wanted it.

"Just go to him." Erin waved me toward her brother.

"If he's happy with her…"

"Trust me, he's not."

"He really isn't." Now Libby piped up from the tent beside Erin's. "He never was. That's why they split in the first place."

They split? Trying to act casual, I turned around to study the blonde. She was clearly comfortable with Adam, touching and pawing him. Oh my god, was that Tracy?

I narrowed my eyes to take her in better. She sure looked different in the sunlight, all gorgeous and tanned, like she just stepped off the plane from the Riviera. Did he bring her to the market in some weak-assed attempt to make me jealous?

Because – damn him – it was working. In all my life, I'd never been jealous of anyone, and yet, here I was, feeling embers of jealousy glowing in my soul. It wasn't a good colour for me.

"I've made it very clear, since the day after—" But I didn't want to admit I'd slept with the guy when I barely knew him even if Erin likely already knew that tidbit of info. "Anyway. He's always known I don't do relationships. There's nothing I can provide. To him or anyone."

"That's a crying shame." Erin put some distance between us as she stood closer to Libby. "Because we know he likes you."

"Likes or liked?" They were two very different things.

"The first one." They both said in sync.

I glanced back over to Adam's tent where Tracy had her hands wrapped around Adam's waist, nuzzling against him. Didn't she have any self-respect? It reeked of desperation. Adam didn't look overly thrilled either, but that was on him.

Erin waved me closer. "Just FYI, you're worth fighting for."

*What?* My jaw dropped. *Fighting for.* In the literal sense.

The pieces, those weird non-sensical pieces, started to fall into place. Had Adam…? No way… it wasn't in him; he'd said as much himself. But still… My gaze wandered back over to his table, and like a magnet, his bandaged hand tugged on my focus.

With a quick nod to the ladies, I stepped to the next vendor and raised my phone, all the while taking quick side glances toward Adam's table.

After taking a few pictures, I went back to my setup and dialled Chloe.

"What's up?"

"We need to talk." I sat in my chair, forcing a smile as a couple of customers wandered by. "He's here with another woman."

It was silent on her end, and I was worried the call had been dropped.

"Oh, by the way, I've seen his hand, Dr. Tarkin."

Her smile was loud and clear on the other end of the line. "I'm almost there."

# Chapter Twenty-Four

H er almost there and mine were not even on the same page. It was nearly thirty minutes before she arrived, and by that time, I had managed to upload the vendors pictures onto the website. However, there were still a few at the back of the market, Adam's included, that I had yet to add.

Chloe sauntered over and immediately plopped into one of the cheap fold-up chairs beside me.

"So, what's up? You've seen Adam?"

I lifted a shoulder, figuring the best way was to ease into the situation. "Sort of. I haven't made it to his table yet. His ex-wife is hanging out with him."

"Oh really?" Her eyes widened, and she leaned back in her chair, craning her neck to see through the crowds to the back. As if, the market was humming.

I tugged on her hand. "Don't hurt yourself. That's her."

The blonde sauntered by, shaking her perfect behind with

each intentional step.

"Her?" Chloe's eyebrows went sky-high.

"Yeah, Miss Perfect over there."

She burst out laughing. "Oh my god, do you hear yourself? You are so jealous."

I lowered my head and barely breathed out the weakest negative.

Chloe's response was unexpected, and she wrapped me in a jovial hug. "Congratulations. It finally happened."

My arms crisscrossed over my chest.

"I never thought I'd see the day when you'd get jealous. Over a guy." She tipped her head back and focused upwards, sending a solid two thumbs up skyward.

"You're crazy." I grabbed my phone as I still had five table pictures to snap. "I asked for help and instead you deliver me this nonsense."

"Kid yourself all you want, deep in your heart, you know it's true."

Yes, I wanted him, and for the fleeting hour on Saturday, I felt it in my heart and soul. That was true happiness, and the best part, it had been returned. Until Tuesday, and that horrific evening.

I lowered my voice. "I saw his hand."

"Even if I knew about the stitches, which I don't–"

"I never said anything about stitches." I narrowed my gaze.

We'd promised no more secrets and had spent several nights opening up to each other. It was refreshing to learn some new things about my best friend.

She brushed her hair off her face. "Patient confidentiality. I can't tell you a thing."

"So, you do know something."

"I know lots. Like there's this amazing path to the beach over there." She pointed in one direction. "But it could be that way. Oh, I'm so mixed up."

"Chloe?" I touched her hand. "Should I ask him?"

She shrugged and leaned back, crossing her legs. "I know what you're hinting at, but if you haven't heard from Officer What's-Her-Name, then I wouldn't. Besides, the injury could be innocent. Could've been woodworking with his sister."

Right? Maybe I was making illogical leaps. Who knew? Maybe Adam did help Erin. That idea wasn't as far-fetched as the ones circulating in my head.

"I should finish taking the pictures."

"Good luck."

In a dash to complete my uploads, I went through the vendors snapping pictures until I finally stopped at Adam's. I avoided all eye contact, and I took in the display of books he had out. Lots of tiny paperbacks, the kind you pocketed for a day on the beach, which was perfect as the day was supposed to be warm and full of sunshine. I held up my phone and blinked as I stared at the image on my screen.

Without me even asking, he posed, but he'd taken better pictures. Everything about his posture and facial expressions lacked excitement.

"Thank you," I managed to squeak out. As much as I tried though, I couldn't stop staring at the sling and bandages.

"Summer?" He reached for my hand, and I stared at our connection, suddenly feeling raw and exposed. Neon signs gave off less illumination than I did as I stood in a puddle of my own nervousness. "I think we–"

"Wait for me." Like a bad smell, the blonde suddenly appeared, snaking her arm around Adam's waist. "Can you get one of the two of us?"

"She only takes the vendors," Adam said to the blonde.

"Well, I'm helping." I wasn't sure about her supposed hyena-like laugh, but her voice was high-pitched, and it instantly grated on my frayed nerves. She held a book like a game show model, her fingers tapping the cover as she lifted it beside her face. "See? You want to read this."

"She's finished." Adam's voice was terse, irritated even, as he directed it at the blonde.

"Thank you. If you'll excuse me," I said, stepping away.

My insides felt like they were going to explode, and it hurt to inhale beyond a shallow breath. It was more than jealousy. This was what a broken heart felt like; that pain was unforgettable.

Chloe met me and draped her arm across my shoulders as we walked back to my station, where I dropped like a sack of flour onto the plastic chair.

"I don't blame you."

I stared at my screen, uploading the most recent pictures.

"What?"

"It's okay to like him."

Avoiding her gaze, I frantically typed, and then hit the backspace button a hundred times to erase the egregious spelling errors. I really needed to focus on what I was doing otherwise all my thoughts were going to be broadcasted across my social media pages.

"He's different, but in a good way."

"You say that all the time."

She took a long sip of her coffee and laughed while customers walked by. "You'd think after a while it would stop getting awkward."

Was she referring to Adam? I wasn't sure, so I twisted to look at her. "What are you talking about?"

She rolled her eyes. "One of my patients walked by and they got a borderline horrified look when they saw me. All of them do that when I'm spotted outside the clinic."

"Probably because you've seen them naked." I refocused my attention, carefully pasting my correctly typed words onto the post, forever thankful the conversation was deflected off me.

"Do you think all my patients have to be in a state of undress when they come in?"

"Not most, but that would make it uncomfortable for them when they see you outside the clinic."

"Perhaps, however, I've seen him naked, and he doesn't act at all strange."

With that, I looked in the direction of the guy she was

referring to. He was cute, in a handsome way. "Clinic or otherwise?"

"Oh god, otherwise." She slapped my arm, and her voice hushed in excitement. "I may have some loose morals when it comes to staffing, but there's no way I'd ever cross that line with a patient. Never. Ever. Ever."

"Good." I stared at the guy who was trying to be casual as he hung around the bike repair shop set up for the market. "Is that Justin?"

"Oh, yeah."

Yep, definitely her type, but younger than I thought. If I had to venture a guess on his age by checking him out, I'd put him in his very late teens. Maybe early twenties.

"The stamina," she said dreamily.

I gave him another glance and resumed my work. "You better be careful."

"I'm double bagging, and I'm on the pill."

"That's not what I meant." I hit publish on my website and leaned back on the cheap plastic chair, tapping my finger against my chin. "Do you think I could plan a wedding?"

She licked her lips and gave a little wave to Justin. "Do I think you could? Yes, absolutely. Do I think you should? No way in hell. Why are you asking?"

"I just got an email inquiring if I'd help coordinate a wedding."

Chloe snorted, took another sip of her coffee, and leaned over to read the email. "I'd say no. Wait, who's it for?"

I covered the screen. "Stop peeking."

"I just want to know who's off the market." She shrugged but kept making side-eye glances at Justin.

I couldn't help but notice the way she was checking him out. Maybe it was more than a sexual attraction. "Trust me, I'm sure they were off the market before you arrived."

She huffed. "They all were."

"Except him." I nodded in Justin's direction.

"Oh, stop." A faint blush crept across her high cheekbones. "He's just a fun toy."

"Tell him that. It's what all guys want to hear." I shuddered violently as a fresh wave of memories from last Tuesday surfaced.

I needed to get them out and instead thought back to the Saturday with Adam. Riding on his motorbike. The wind in my face. Feeling safe, invincible even. For a heartbeat, I'd gotten a glimpse of happiness I'd never thought I'd have again.

Chloe rubbed my back. "You're thinking about him, aren't you?"

I blinked a few times and clicked over to another tab. "No, of course not."

"Yeah, well, your face says otherwise. You really need to tell him what's in your heart."

Customers walked by in droves, and the chatter was music to my ears. The vendors should be happy.

My own happiness was moot. "What's the point? It's not like we're anything. We're barely even friends now. He saw me with that jerk, and now he's back with his ex-wife."

"Yeah, keep telling yourself that. Let me know how it works out for you."

I cocked an eyebrow. It wasn't as manicured as hers, but I could raise it higher. We proved that one Friday night.

"You should go for it. You know he's smitten with you." Her smile was so large, mega-watt wouldn't even describe it.

"I don't know it. Not anymore. And neither do you."

"You'll never know if you don't try. Go and talk to him." Chloe rose from her seat. "It's time to get back on the proverbial horse. You're due, and he's clearly ready for the challenge."

"And what challenge would that be?"

She sighed but gently squeezed my shoulder in a big sisterly way. "I love you, and I say this with the biggest heart, but don't pass up this chance out of fear and miscommunication. You'll lose, and you'll regret it forever. I speak from experience."

"What?" I've known Chloe for nearly a decade, and although she's a few years older, I don't ever recall her having passed up an opportunity with any guy. No guy was dumb enough to turn her down.

However, it was clear from the dismissive way she wove her hands through the air that the topic was closed. "I'm going to go check out things back there and see if anything tickles my fancy."

I scanned the immediate area. Justin had disappeared. "Have fun."

"That's my plan."

She walked away, blending in seamlessly into the growing crowd, and I dove back into the collection of accumulating emails and checking my social media notifications. A while later, Chloe dropped off her car keys so I could get home, as she left on Justin's right arm, a huge smile on her face. I was happy she'd found someone, even if she thought it was temporary, it did put a spring in her step. Justin was a lucky guy.

As the market wound down, the vendors packed up and left, adding their tables and chairs to the cart, and saving me a ton of extra work.

Adam, unable to collapse the tents, had enlisted a few other guys to do so and directed them to stack the bags near the entrance. One by one as the job finished, they left, leaving Adam and me alone in the parking lot.

Where was the rental company?

"You don't have to wait. I've got this." I scanned the horizon, searching in earnest for the big, lumbering truck.

"As if I'd leave you alone."

I faced him, but my gaze was drawn to the bandaged hand.

"About last week."

I put my hand up to stop him. "If it's about payback, please email me the cost of the tickets and any expenses that went along with it, I'm happy to repay you."

I'd never seen eyes widen so much.

"Is that what you think this is about?" He carved his hands through his hair, holding his hand behind his head for a moment before releasing it.

"Isn't it?"

He slumped against the top of a folded tent. "God, you are the most stubborn person I've ever met."

"Yep." It was the strongest response I had in my arsenal, and it wasn't that strong.

His fingertips scratched at the day-old scruff along his jawline. "All I wanted was to check in with you. To see if you are okay?"

I pulled my shoulders back and retrieved some hidden strength and confidence. "Yeah, I'm fine. I should be asking if you're okay?"

He kicked at the blades of grass and blew out a long breath. "It's a long story."

Prickles of energy danced along my spine, twisting, and turning until they reached my fingertips. I grabbed my clipboard and fought to control my hands. All my checkmarks were scribbles, rather than neat marks.

"Summer stop."

I froze.

The air crackled.

"I care about you."

Shit, Chloe, Erin, Libby – they were all right, and despite my protests to the contrary, a swarm of butterflies took flight in the excitement. "What about Tracy?"

"My non-committal ex-wife, who thinks she can show up in

my life and act like nothing's wrong? That because some time has passed, I'll forgive her and let her back in? Because she'd rather be with me than single."

"You're a nice enough guy." Despite the incessant pounding of my heart, it had clearly not pumped enough oxygen to my brain.

"Nice enough?" He chuckled, but maybe in a weak attempt to lighten the mood. "This may come as a bit of a surprise, but I have some standards, and too bad for Tracy, but she doesn't reach them anymore." He stepped closer, the gap between us shrinking rapidly. "I do care about you, and I'm worried about you, so worried."

"I… ah…" I breathed him in, relishing his intoxicating scent.

His steely blue gaze stabbed at the walls I'd kept sky-high around my heart. His expression truly held concern as he stood directly in front of me. He was close enough to touch. All I had to do to raise my hand and lay it on his chest.

"There's a damn good reason I didn't return your calls."

I stepped back, shaking my head, cohesive letters failing to blend into real words.

"I found Kyle."

# Chapter Twenty-Five

O f course, as soon as Adam dropped the bomb on me, that's when the rental company decided to arrive.

The white cube van rocketed back and forth as it travelled down the curving, gravel road.

"Wait." I put my hand on his chest and involuntarily groaned from the touch. "Please don't leave."

"I'm not going anywhere."

I searched his deep blue eyes for the truth I already knew in my heart. "I know, and I appreciate that."

Once the rentals were gone, it was just the two of us, but the place didn't seem like the best place to have a heart-to-heart.

"Can we go somewhere and talk?" I asked, praying he'd agree, but since he hadn't left yet...

"Where would you like to go?"

"Glass beach."

I had one move left. One thing I could do to show Adam all

was not completely lost, especially when it came to me. Thing was, it scared me more than anything to do it.

Straddling a thick log stretched out across the sandy portion of the beach, I kicked at the sand beneath my feet, making little dugouts. It was the only way to channel my nervous energy.

"I have so many questions to ask, but I don't know which to ask first."

"Before you say anything, can I start?" Adam inched closer, holding his arm tight to his chest as he moved.

I swallowed and slowly nodded.

"I'm not here to talk to you about what you said or did. Figure there's no point, you'll just shut down." His gaze shifted between my eyes. "However, first things first. Are. You. Okay?"

I tore my gaze from his warmth and stared out at the coolness of the ocean. There were various levels of *okay*, and if I was honest with myself, I hadn't yet reached the second level. Yes, I was working on putting my life back together, ethically and morally, as my own hypocrisy slapped me in the face daily, but as for me wholly? If I was going to make this work, honesty had to come first. No more hiding.

"No." I closed my eyes and wrapped my arms tightly around my chest, trying desperately to hold myself together. "I am not okay."

Adam continued to run his hand up and down my back,

holding me close until the birds settled their chirps and the sky faded into rich mauves and violets. When my sobs punctured the still air with a heartbreaking cry from fear of what could've been, he held me tighter. Never spoke a word, and never left my side either.

When my tears finally stopped, and my breathing returned to a less laboured variety, I took inventory of my situation but tried not to read more into it than it was. I needed to stick to the facts.

Adam was truly a great guy; warm and genuine.

He pushed a little, but not forcefully.

And… he'd silently hung out with me while I buckled under self-hatred and heartache.

However, it was also the first time in a long time I'd shared space with someone who didn't try to solve my problems or try to piece me back together, and who didn't try to fill it with trite and meaningless conversation. Even Chloe had never managed that.

It was nice and welcome, and felt perfectly natural. Adam had become my safe space.

And Chloe was right. I'd be a fool to walk away from this without even trying.

I broke the easy peace with a hoarse whisper as I swiped my palms over my eyes. "Thank you."

With a gentle caress of his finger, he brushed the stray hairs off my face and searched my eyes. "For what?"

"For this. For not giving up on me. Not completely, anyway." My gaze fell to his arm. "Although I think I may already know the answer to this, I need to ask anyway." I inhaled a deep breath of ocean air, holding it in before I let it go. "Kyle."

"That's not a question." A small smirk teased his lips.

But I didn't share his gentle attempt to lighten the situation. "Is your arm damaged because of Kyle?"

I expected him to look away and deflect with a wry joke or comment.

Instead, he cupped my chin and stroked my cheek with his thumb. "You don't have to worry about him anymore."

Fresh tears streamed down my cheek and pooled in his palm. I rolled my bottom lip between my teeth to stop it from quivering.

"I'll spare you the details, but after you left that night, it dawned on me who he was. By the time I figured it out, because I was a little slow on the uptake, the accident had occurred, and you were being treated on scene."

"You were there?" Although the details after I hit my head were a little fuzzy, I don't recall seeing him anywhere near the ambulance.

His head bobbed. "I heard the snippets of conversations and got close enough to hear you tell the EMT what had happened."

I broke eye contact and stared at the sand watching as a tiny crab shuffled sideways to hide under a rock.

"It wasn't your fault."

"If I hadn't made the deal to begin with." The crab scuttled back out, capturing my attention, because I didn't want to dare take a look at his face and see his expression.

"No." Adam's strong tone punctured the air and he put a

finger over my lips. "No. You are not to blame for Kyle's actions."

I held my breath.

"He's the loser, okay?"

My lips failed to move.

Adam breathed, and slowly tipped his head from side to side. "I waited outside the police station for you. I couldn't – wouldn't – I refused to leave you alone."

"You watched me, like a stalker?" I wasn't sure if I was floored by his dedication, or totally creeped out. Regardless, it was an interesting emotion to know he'd been there.

"To make sure you made it back to the apartment safely. After all, Kyle was still roaming around. Somewhere."

I sighed. At least he didn't know about the fallout in the police station between Chloe and me, or about my night of restless napping on the beach.

His hand fell to my knee, but he didn't caress it any higher. Had he sensed apprehension? "I know you well enough to know you wouldn't accept help, but I couldn't leave you stranded either."

My heart pounded harder, and I blinked away a fresh set of tears as his face contorted and his lips moved.

"That night, I camped out on the beach too. You couldn't see me, but I made sure you weren't in any danger. Since I knew you wouldn't accept my help, I enlisted Amber, nudging her to check out the beach."

Thunder rolled in the distance and dark clouds swept across the horizon.

"You did that? Did you pay for it all too?" Despite what Mona has said, someone had to have paid for my stay at the B&B.

He shook his head. "That was all on Amber, her heart is bigger than her wallet and her wallet is considerable. I just wanted her to give you something warm to drink, and to get you off the beach before the cops found you. It was Amber who contacted Mona."

"And Mona told you?"

A weak smile formed. "She kept tabs on you on my behalf, and likely hers too, and reported in with any changes. Except there weren't any as you didn't leave the B&B."

I shrugged.

"I suspected it was because of a safety issue—"

"It was more of a *I-need-to-sort-my-life-out* issue. Lawyers, bankers, finding a job." My breath shuddered in my chest. "I tried calling you, and I texted you repeatedly."

"I know."

Another roll of thunder, way out in the sea, however, tiny chilly drops of rain announced the arrival of an incoming storm.

"So why did you ignore me? How could you follow me around like a nice stalker but not respond to me, especially when I reached out to you?"

"Because I did what the cops didn't prioritize."

"What was that?" My heart plunged into my gut and stopped beating for a moment.

"I found the bastard."

The air froze around me, and my gaze fell from his soulful

eyes to his hand. "So, you did do what I think you did."

He wet his lips, rolling them quickly between his teeth. "Let's just say I was making amends."

"To me?" Because it didn't make any sense.

"Partly, yes, but also to Erin. Years ago, I didn't protect her, and because of my actions, she has Vera." His Adam's apple bobbed. "I vowed I wouldn't let it happen again to any woman, let alone someone I loved."

Like the Grinch at Christmas, my heart grew two sizes.

"But it almost did. With you. And it gutted me. What that bastard was going to do." His voice darkened with a growl. "So, I went off the grid, if you will. It was surprisingly easy to find him. I actually expected more of a hunt, and I was a little disappointed that there wasn't." He shook his head. "Regardless, when we met up, I dealt with him. And spent the night in jail."

"For me?" I couldn't believe someone would care enough about me to not put me in harm's way. In fact, he put himself through the wringer to protect me, and spent time in the slammer because of it.

A wash of crimson flushed over his face, and as quickly it ebbed away. "I'm the kind of guy who will fight for your honour, and I want to be the hero you were getting in Andre"

How did he know about him? I'd kept that under lock and key. "How? How do you know about him?"

"It doesn't matter how I found out, but I think it would be good for us – for you – to tell me about him. I think it'll help me understand the big picture." His tone was soft, encouraging, as was the warmth on his face. There was truth in his words.

"You really want to know?"

"I do." He held my hand with both of his, giving it a tender squeeze.

The wind whistled in the nearby trees and in the distance a foghorn rumbled. Even the encroaching darkness of a storm had a soothing feel to it, and I allowed that peacefulness to settle into my soul before I ripped it wide open.

I punctured the silence with a heartbreaking statement. "Andre was my fiancé."

Adam didn't move – not a lip quiver, not a twitch of the eye, not even a throat swallow.

My shoes dug into the wet sand. "Andre and I were high school sweethearts, some would say since we'd been an item since grade ten. He was my first everything." As in *everything*. "We studied in university together."

"Was he going to be an event planner too?"

I gently laughed, and it lightened my pain. Marginally. "No. No one really studies to be that. At least I don't think so." The wind blew my hair into my face, obstructing my view of Adam, so I snapped my head to free my view. "We were both in education."

"Teaching is a noble profession."

"I agree. He wanted to make a difference in the lives of little kids, whereas I wanted to teach the older ones. But still." A memory floated to the front of my brain; one I hadn't reflected on in years.

Just seeing Andre's smiling face formed another crevice in my heart. "We got engaged in our second year of university. Totally romantic, and I'll spare you the details." I waved my hand through the air. It was enough to give the Cliff Notes version, he didn't need – or deserve – an essay. "Life was perfect. Or so I thought."

A dull ache was forming and the food I'd just eaten was turning into a lead weight.

"Toward the end of our second year, Andre started getting sick. A lot. So many doctors' appointments and rushed visits to the ER." The unforgettable stabbing sensation punctured fresh holes back in my heart. "Cancer, they said. Pancreatic. From diagnosis to the funeral was less than three months."

"Wow. That's quick." He stared at me, sympathy rolling off him like the waves moving on the beach.

"It was. So quick. Devastatingly quick." I inhaled a calming breath of salty ocean air, letting it hover in my lungs before exhaling long and slow. "I dropped out of college. Couldn't hack being there, didn't want to go into the profession we'd dreamed we'd have until retirement. I moved in with Chloe while she was finishing med school." Somehow, just talking about Andre lifted a tiny weight from my shoulders and allowed a sliver of sunshine in. It had been too long. Far too long.

"How'd you end up being an event planner?"

I scooted back higher on the log and pulled my legs up around me. "Stupid, really. I wanted menial work, hard back breaking work, anything to take my mind off Andre, so I started working at an event rentals company, first as a loader, and then I moved into the showroom where I was helping people get what they needed, and don't tell my former boss, but I was sending them to other places where the things were cheaper. A customer said I should be an event planner since I really seemed to have an eye for detail and knowledge of the best pricing. So, I looked into it and joined a startup company."

"On Demand, I take it?" He shifted on the log, propping one leg up and letting the other dig into the sand.

"Yep. Declan started pretty close to the same time as me, and we just hit it off." I inhaled and released a big sigh. "We became good friends, but that was all it was. It was all I could ever give him."

In the far distance, a rumble of thunder crossed the horizon, and a cool gust of wind followed.

Adam stared out into the horizon. "And you've never had a relationship since?"

"Crazy, right? Never met anyone I'd give my heart to." Until now. I swallowed as the truth lit up my heart like the lightning in the distance. "My heart belonged to Andre."

"Belonged?"

Yeah, I heard it too. What did that mean? I glanced up to the heavens as tears blurred my view. Was he giving me permission to move on?

"How long has it been?" Adam cleared his throat. "Since he died, I mean?"

I swallowed the solid lump in the back of my throat. It plunged like a stone in the water into the depths of my stomach.

"Seven years."

His head bobbed. "That's like, what, a quarter of your life?"

*Wow.* I'd never thought about it that way, but he was right. Andre had been *gone* for twenty-five percent of my life. Our time together had even been less than that – only five years.

He clasped his hands together and stared at them. "I'm just going to throw this out into the air, so take it as you will. Do you think Andre would want you to be lonely?"

"Oh, I'm not lonely. I have Chloe and my job."

"I mean in here." Slowly, his hand moved through the narrowed space between us until he tapped just below my shoulder, right above my heart.

The weight of what he was asking pressed on my shoulders, and I had no answer.

"You don't have to respond, but it's something to think about." He inhaled and ran his fingers through his hair. "Since we're being forthcoming and revealing, maybe I should take some of the pressure off you and tell you about my ex-wife. If you want to know."

I inched closer and leaned my head toward him, loving how open and honest we were being, and how the fear of sharing what had gripped me my whole life was so frightening. Not with Adam. "Yes, I do."

The lightning flashed in the distance once more, and the waves on the beach rolled with a little more intensity.

Giving him my full attention, I inched closer and tipped my head.

"Tracy and I were married fresh out of high school. She was barely eighteen, and I was almost nineteen. We were friends, who fell into lust, and thought the next logical step was marriage. We were young and foolish and had these wild ideas of making it big in the city." He pulled on his face with both hands. "But then Grandpa died, and I inherited the shop, so our plans for moving away stalled. She wanted a family, but we weren't able; some kind of blockage in one of her tubes. The tension between us grew, and somewhere along the way, we just stopped loving the other, although I'd say it was her who stopped first." He rose and began pacing in the sand. "However, and this is the crazy part so bear with me, even after she moved away from me, I couldn't help but follow her. Not physically, but maybe akin to internet stalking."

My eyes widened. I had no idea, although based on all the information he suddenly knew about me from the video to the letter Declan had sent, it shouldn't have been a surprise.

"Because you still love her."

He shrugged. "Maybe in the past tense." He shook his head and broke our connection. "I kept tabs on her – her social media was wide open, almost as if she just didn't care. She'd been out with many, many guys, and even moved in with one for a month. She lived in Qualicum Beach for a while, but now she's back."

"In Cheshire Bay?"

"Stewart Surf."

"And she was going to be on the yacht?"

"Apparently. Amber had been keeping light tabs on her too."

He huffed and huddled under his jacket as a gust of ocean air blew across the beach.

"And today?"

He shook his head, and a glimmer of despair stretched between his ears. "Yeah, well, we all make mistakes. We ran into each other last night and, well, one drunken thing led to another, and she spent the night."

"Oh. I'm sorry." I didn't know what else to say.

"There's nothing to be sorry for. You didn't cause it. I was weak and feeling out of sorts. For a minute, she offered companionship. It wasn't her I wanted, but it was her I settled for."

"No one should ever settle for another person." I cast my focus out to the endless sea. "Are you lonely?" I threw his question back at him. "In here." Turning, I touched his muscled chest and a flurry of hyper butterflies zoomed in my gut.

"Well, I have Erin and Francesca and Harrison, and all my friends." Once again, he straddled the log and inched closer with an effortless smirk building. "But to answer your question honestly – yes, yes I am."

I swallowed and shivered.

With a gentle caress of his finger, he swiped the stray hairs off my face and searched my eyes. "It's probably totally cliché, but I'm the kind of guy who wants to share his life with someone. To have the same interests as another. To share space without the need for talking. I just want to enjoy being with another woman. A beautiful woman with a beautiful heart."

"And you think that's me?"

"I know it is. You just need to believe in it yourself." He reached for my hand and cradled it between his. "If it's what you want."

Tingles danced across the back of my neck and possible responses dissolved in my head.

Adam's gaze reached the depth of my soul, both with his words and the soothing way he spoke. "I appreciate you being so upfront with me, about all your reasonings for not dating, and I understand the hesitancy. But I want to try, and I want you to try with me. I'm willing to let you lead and call the shots."

"What if..."

He covered my lips with his finger. "No, what ifs."

"But seriously. What if I hurt you because I put the brakes on because I'm not ready? I don't want a replay of..." I glanced into his warm, affectionate eyes.

"Then it's on me, and I'll back off, but I'm not leaving."

"But–"

"Damn girl, give a guy a chance," he said with a smile and a tender squeeze of my hand. "I know I'm not Andre, and I know I never will be. But the truth of the matter is he's gone, and you're still alive. And I'm still alive. You're messed up, I'm messed up, but maybe together we make sense."

"Even if I'm scared?"

"I'll be there to hold your hand. I'm willing to slay your dragons; I'll just need to see which one takes priority."

Tears of gratitude broke through and rendered me speechless.

"Thank you, for slaying all my dragons," I whispered as my heart hammered louder than the rolling thunder. My focus danced between his eyes and lowered over his whisker cheeks to settle on his plump pout. "Can I try something?"

He nodded, and I inched myself even closer as the air between us warmed while the ocean breeze wrapped around our perfect little bubble. My hands trembled as I cupped his cheeks and stretched out my neck to navigate the unfamiliar territory.

Responding in expectation, he gingerly tipped his head but kept a locked focus on my eyes.

With a deliberate motion, I erased the gap and sealed us together, my breath catching as our lips brushed together. Pressing harder, I opened to him, allowing a teasing tongue to slip its way into mine. Beneath my palms, his cheeks heated, and I tossed my arms around his neck, pulling him even tighter against my body as I threaded my fingers through his hair. I welcomed him in, and our slow dance began tenderly, turning into a heady mixture of movements that weakened my knees. It also set my soul on fire.

Needing a moment to breathe, I pulled back and rested my forehead against him. "You're a great kisser, dragon slayer."

"Is that my nickname now?" He planted a kiss on top of my nose. "And you're okay?"

I took him in before brushing my lips over his once more. A joyful smile bubbled out of me as my heart pounded out the perfect melody. "I'm okay. Better than okay. Honestly."

I nodded and stared at the amazing man in front of me. Tipping my head from side to side, I studied his face, and trailed a gaze over his chest, down to his wounded hand. The damage he took because of me. I still couldn't believe it.

"We'll go slow, take it one day at a time." He grabbed my hand, and pressed his lips into the palm, rolling it up. "I promise."

The thunder rumbled, growing stronger as it reached the shore, and with it, came the tapping of cool raindrops.

"And as much as I'd like to stay, I think we should consider leaving."

"Of course."

He caressed the side of my face. "Stay the night with me?"

A broad smile filled my face. "I'd like that."

He hopped off the log and extended his hand. "We'll go as fast or slow as you dictate."

The raindrops made craters in the sand.

Sliding my fingers through his, I pulled him to a stop. "Wait. I want to say…" I took a deep breath. "Thank you. For believing in me."

"Some things are worth it, and you are one of them."

# Epilogue

*Two months later*

I stopped in front of the wood carver's set up, curious to see which exquisite, hand-carved decorations and pictures she'd brought to the market this week. They were remarkable in their detail, and I figured she could easily fetch more than her asking price. Typically, Erin went home with an empty truck and a fat wallet.

She stopped her set up and posed, hand on her latest piece – a whale, its tail high in the air. "What do you think?"

"Be sure to show Landon over there, as he's one of the whale expedition tour guides."

She smiled warmly. "Oh, he knows."

I nodded, pleased that they'd already made the connection, and from the way she said it, maybe they had made more than just a connection. Landon's tour company was a recent addition to Bayside Market, and something Adam and I said we had to check out.

"Well, that's great."

She rearranged a few smaller pieces on the table to accommodate the whale. "How's that piece working out for you?"

Not long after Adam and I got together permanently, I purchased one of her most sought-after pieces, she called it *Sorrowful Regret*. It was a woman grieving; a piece she'd showcased a few weeks back. It spoke volumes to me, and it had to have been destiny for it to still be available for purchase since no one else had bought it. Or maybe, as Adam had suggested, she jacked the price so no one *could* buy it as he'd thought she'd made it especially for me.

Erin continued to smile, one of those I'd-like-to-get-back-to-work smiles, so I moved on to the next booth.

Chloe meandered next to me. "So… Justin got his acceptance letter."

Justin was Chloe's much younger boyfriend, young enough to be finally heading off to university after two gap years.

"Kind of late, isn't it?" I fanned my tank top.

It was July and the sweltering heat made my clothes stick to my skin. Thank goodness there were tents for the vendors; it would be brutal to bake in the sun all day.

"It was a last-minute choice."

"And where's Justin going? UBC or Vic?" I stopped at the next vendor, who was always short on small talk. A quick pose, a thank you, and we were off.

"U of T."

My jaw dropped. "As in University of Toronto?"

She nodded.

"That's across the country."

"I know."

"Wow, I'm sorry."

She hung out beside me casually inspecting the previous vendor's wares while I kept snapping photos. I'd capped out at thirty vendors a week. It was manageable, and now that I'd developed a nice rhythm, it didn't consume my free time. I had time to work my custodial job and pay down my hovering debt, which will likely take years to clean up, but it was better than declaring bankruptcy – an idea I'd strongly flirted with. But the most important aspect of having free time was being able to spend it with my own personal dragon slayer. I couldn't wait to get over to his table. Three more vendors to go.

"You don't seem too upset about him leaving."

She shrugged. "I guess I hadn't ever seen a long-term with him. He was more a–"

When she stopped talking, I faced her. She had paled considerably, as if she'd seen a ghost, and was staring down the strip of vendors.

"Chloe, what's wrong?"

She grabbed my arm, as if hanging on for dear life. "Who's running... that table? The one with ... the books?"

"Adam." But she knew that.

"Not him, the other guy. There." She pointed at the table beside Adam, her finger twitching.

"Oh, that's BJ Sutcliff, our local author of the week. Have

you read his stuff?" Judging by the look on her face, I'd wager a strong no.

She shook her head. "First name Benjamin by any chance?"

I flipped my gaze over to him, and then casually back to Chloe. "Could be. I think his form just said BJ." With Justin being out of the picture, at least soon, there was a new possibility of fresh meat. I nudged her arm. "He's kind of cute, don't you think?"

"What's not to admire? The thick locks of dark wavy hair, the scruff across his cheeks and chin. His lean build with broad shoulders, and dark eyes, highlighted with long lashes."

"Oh my god, you can see his eyelashes?" I leaned my head forward and pinched my eyes together to focus better.

"I just know. It goes with the type. Probably drives a high-end sports car, and wears clothes that reek of old, stale money. No doubt if you don't conform to his brand of perfection, you won't last long."

"Do you not like him? Is he a horrible patient or something?"

"You never mentioned anything about him."

I stepped over to the next vendor after scrunching my face at Chloe. "I've never really discussed who was here. Honestly, I didn't think you cared that much." I readied my camera for the vendor, and he smiled, holding up one of his wares. "Thank you."

Chloe almost seemed to huddle behind me.

"What's going on? How do you know BJ?"

I didn't think it was possible for her to pale even further, but she did. "I need to go home. I'm sorry I can't stay to help. I didn't know him as BJ, but as Benji."

"Benji? What a sec?" My eyes went large as saucers. "As in GiGi... the guy you claimed was the love of your life?" Whenever I asked for more info on who GiGi was, she kept her lips sealed tightly, and always twisted the conversation away from him. "Why don't you go say hi?"

She was frozen on the spot, and I had to nudge her to get her to move.

"I can't..."

Chloe may have lost her will to move, but BJ hadn't. Gaze targeted on my best friend, he maneuvered himself out from between the tables, and when I turned to face Chloe, she was gone.

BJ sidled up beside me, scanning the crowd. "God, she looks fantastic. That was Chloe York, wasn't it?"

York, a name she used to go by. Professionally, she used her birth mother's name - Tarkin. However, I wasn't going to say anything. It wasn't my place.

"Was it something I said?" BJ stood there, arms hanging limply at his side.

I couldn't see how. There was a story there, something Chloe had kept hidden for years, but the lid was open to her Pandora's box, and suddenly, I needed to know more about the man who'd once held my best friend's heart. "Tell me how you know Chloe?"

"Maybe you should get the rest of the information from her."

Oh, hell yeah, Chloe and I were going to have a long conversation indeed.

# Dear Reader

Wow – what happened between Chloe and BJ? There's always so much going on in Cheshire Bay, I'm just never fully ready to leave it when the story is done. Hopefully, you aren't either, as I have some amazing stories in this series. Next up is Chloe's, followed by Erin's and then Libby's. It's going to be awesome.

Summer's story was hard to pull out of her, and yes, as authors we have constant conversations with our characters, LOL. She was just as secretive to me as she was to Chloe and Adam, but beneath all her layers was a beautiful soul, she just needed to find the person who believed in her and allowed her true light to shine. I hope you enjoyed Summer's story as much as I did getting it all out.

As an author, it makes my day when a reader or blogger shares their thoughts and gives me feedback on the characters they've invested their time in. When readers fall in love with a character or a series, it's encouraging to write more. So, if you don't mind, share with me what you liked, what you loved, or even what you hated. I'd love a rating/review on your favourite retailer site. It doesn't have to be long, even just as simple as *"Couldn't put it down"* or *"Loved the characters"* or *"Why isn't Cheshire Bay a real place?"* works. Reviews and ratings help me gain visibility, and as I'm sure you can tell from my books, reviews are tough to come by. If you have the time for an extra review, here's my author page on Goodreads .

Thank you so much for spending time with me.

Yours,

H.M. Shander

# Other Romantic Reads by H.M. Shander

Duly Noted

That Summer

If You Say Yes

Serving Up Innocence

Serving Up Devotion

Serving Up Secrecy

Serving Up Hope

It All Began with a Note

It All Began with a Mai-Tai

It All Began with a Wedding

Noel

Whistler's Night

Dreamers in Cheshire Bay

Return to Cheshire Bay

Adrift in Cheshire Bay

Awake in Cheshire Bay

Christmas in Cheshire Bay

Journey to Cheshire Bay

Charmed in Cheshire Bay

Second Chances in Cheshire Bay

Unforgiven in Cheshire bay

Flirty in Cheshire Bay

Full listings available at www.hmshander.com

# acknowledgements

Writing these thank yous never gets easier – NEVER – as I'm always afraid I'll miss someone, or a category will be left out. And then I wonder, does anyone even read these? I know as an author, I do, but do readers?

Writing a book for the most part, is a solo endeavor, but I could not have this ready for you to read if not for the cheerleading and support of some magnificent people in my life.

First – my Shander family -. Thank you for giving me the countless hours I needed to complete this. For all your encouragement. For your excitement in returning to markets and author readings. I hope one day I will make you as proud of me as I am of you.

To my parents and in-laws and extended family. Thank you for your cheerleading and encouraging your friends to give my stories a read. Who knew bad when I struggled so much in English class that I'd find a way to express myself?

To my wonderfully dedicated alpha reader – Mandy. Thanks for being my go-to gal. To chat through ideas, to help me see the big picture, the nitty-gritty, and everything in between. I love how we started out as authors willing to help each other out, and now we are friends having zoom chats and sharing bits of our lives. I'm grateful for your friendship.

To my critique partner- Josephine. Over and over I redid a few of those chapters, changing them from boring reads into ones with the conflict it needed to keep it interesting. Thanks for your help in bringing that out. Summer is a more layered person thanks to your help.

To my cover designer – Eleanor. OMG. You've designed yet another BEAUTIFUL cover. All the Cheshire Bay covers have your touch, but I just love what you did with this one. The green colouring, the new font colour – all tie back to Summer and her quest for money and fame. Love it!

To my editor – Irina. I'd like to think I'm getting better, but seeing all the track changes, maybe not so much. Or maybe, I'm just keeping you on your toes and finding all new things to mess up. Hahah. Appreciate all your arduous work and for slipping this in between assignments and a never-ending pile of schoolwork. You rock.

If I missed you, it certainly wasn't intentional. I know I couldn't be where I am without the help of so many others. Thank you! And thank you for reading and making it all the way to the end. You all rock.

# about the author

USA TODAY bestselling author H.M. Shander is a stargazing, romantic at heart who once attended Space Camp and wanted to pilot the space shuttle, not just any STS – specifically Columbia. However, the only shuttle she operates in her real world is the #momtaxi; a reliable electric car that transports her two kids to school, work and various sporting events. When she's not commandeering Elektra, you can find the elementary school librarian surrounded by classes of children as she reads the best storybooks in multiple voices. After she's tucked her endearing kids into bed and kissed her trophy husband goodnight, she moonlights as a contemporary romance novelist; the writer of sassy heroines and sweet, swoon-worthy heroes who find love in the darkest of places.

For all the latest release news, subscribe to H.M. Shander's newsletter, or you can follow her on Twitter(@HM_Shander), Facebook (hmshander), or check out her website at www.hmshander.com.

Thanks for reading– all the way to the very end.

www.ingramcontent.com/pod-product-compliance
Lightning Source LLC
Chambersburg PA
CBHW031952240626
47153CB00003B/962